About the Author

Loree Westron grew up in North Central Idaho and now lives on the south coast of the UK. Her short stories and literary criticism have been published in journals and anthologies, including *The London Magazine* and the *Los Angeles Review of Books*. She has a PhD in Creative Writing. *Missing Words* is her debut work of longer fiction.

Missing Words

LOREE WESTRON

Fairlight Books

First published by Fairlight Books 2021

Fairlight Books
Summertown Pavilion, 18–24 Middle Way, Oxford, OX2 7LG

A CIP catalogue record for this book is available from the
British Library

1 2 3 4 5 6 7 8 9 10

ISBN 978-1-912054-03-9

www.fairlightbooks.com

Printed and bound in Great Britain by Clays Ltd.

Designed by Sara Wood

Illustrated by Sam Kalda

This is a work of fiction. Names, characters, business, events
and incidents are the products of the author's imagination.
Any resemblance to actual persons, living or dead, or actual
events is purely coincidental.

To my mother, Karen, with love.

I

She finds him sprawled across the sofa when she returns home from work, his long legs splayed untidily in front of him. Two empty cans of Special Brew and a half-eaten plate of congealed Vesta curry on the floor tell her he has been there for some time.

From the doorway, Jenny gazes in at the scene and hesitates by the light switch. The curtains are pulled closed against the glare of the afternoon sun and the room is dim, almost dark, but she resists putting on the light as she enters. The television is on as usual, filling the room with twilight.

'Short day?'

Simon doesn't look up as she manoeuvres around his legs to sit beside him. His gaze remains fixed on the television. *The Evening News*. Of course. It has become his obsession in the past few months.

'Yeah. It's Friday. Same as last week. And the week before that.'

On the screen, a man in a grey suit stares back at them as he reports on the day's events. 'More than a thousand women have been removed from the Greenham Common peace camp, but leaders say their protests will continue until all nuclear weapons are withdrawn.'

Jenny settles into the cushions, stretches and yawns. 'It's all right for some. Meanwhile I'm doing all the overtime I can get.' She cringes at her half-intended jibe. It's not Simon's fault the MOD is making cutbacks at the dockyard.

The television camera shifts away from the man in the suit to a scene outside the airbase. Signs draped across the perimeter fence read *No Nukes are Good Nukes* and *STOP the Cruise to Genocide*. Police are dragging women from the camp: grandmothers in twinsets and wellington boots, young mums brandishing photographs of their children. Some struggle and kick out as they are carried away. Others go limp.

Simon shakes his head and huffs noisily at the images on the screen. 'Those bloody women ought to be locked up. Bunch of lezzies, I bet.'

The picture changes to the polished black door of Number 10. 'Meanwhile, at Downing Street, the Prime Minister issues a strong rebuke to Welsh miners, and warns union leaders she will not relent.' Hair and pearls in place, Mrs Thatcher steps over the threshold to face a throng of reporters.

Simon mutes the volume with the remote control before the Prime Minister has begun to speak. Jenny's body stiffens in the silence.

'Can't stand that woman's voice,' he mutters to himself.

Jenny rests her head against the back of the sofa. *Politics!* How she hates it. Both sides as bad as each other. Both sides desperate to have the upper hand. She lets her gaze drift round the room and it settles for a moment on a photograph of her father, when he was much younger than she is now. His smile reassures her, and she relaxes again and breathes.

'Just found out that Roger's retiring at the end of the month.' She turns to Simon, hopeful of a response. 'Remember him from the work's do last Christmas? Tall, skinny bloke with a tash. He's moving to Australia to be closer to his grandkids.'

Simon continues to stare at the television in silence.

She tries again. 'It'll be good for him to be with his family. He's been lonely since his wife died.' She looks for signs that her husband is listening. Finding none, she follows the light from the television as it flickers across the faces of Charlotte and Sophie, freckled from the summer sun. *Is it three years ago those pictures were taken? No,* she thinks. *It must be four. Their last proper holiday together. Torquay.*

'So. Where's Charlotte gone off to?' She does not turn to look at Simon for fear her face will betray her. She has waited as long as she could to ask the question, and is trying her best to sound casual and unconcerned. In the two years since Sophie's death, she has nearly perfected the semblance of *calm*.

'She's with a mate from college.' His voice is flat, almost dismissive. 'Marilyn or Marianne or something. And Ian.'

Ian. Jenny closes her eyes and counts to ten.

'But do you know where they are?' she asks, then before he can answer, 'Did she say when she'd be home?' She feels the panic welling up in her throat and clenches her jaw to rein it under control.

'Look,' he says softly, 'she'll be nineteen in a couple of weeks, and off to university soon after that. You can't keep track of her every minute. You need to give her a bit of space.'

Jenny winces at the mention of Charlotte's birthday. She wishes she could let the date pass by as though it were any other day of the year.

'She's been working hard all week, and now it's Friday night.' His voice is measured and impassive. 'She's gone out with friends and she'll be back late. It's what kids do. And yes, I made sure she has money for a taxi to get home. You have to stop worrying so much about her, Jen. You'll end up driving her away if you don't.'

Her eyes drift back to the photographs on the wall. She takes a breath and lets her eyes rest on Sophie. She was such a sweet-natured girl. A joy to be around. A pleasure. If there was one moment she could go back to, it would be then. Everything about their lives had been perfect that summer. Jenny closes her eyes and lets the memories wash over her. If only she had understood then, how quickly time passes.

How quickly things can change and disappear. She would have tried harder to keep her younger daughter close.

When she opens her eyes again, her gaze has shifted to the left. To Charlotte. Now she has certainly changed in the past four years. She's nearly grown, Jenny thinks. Nearly nineteen. *How is that even possible?*

'We should do something special for Charlotte's birthday, this year.' She glances at Simon. 'We could go out for a meal. Invite Mother. Make a proper celebration of it. What do you think?' His eyes don't waver from the television screen. 'Si?'

Yes. A celebration. Maybe this year she could make a birthday cake again. Something special with piped roses, perhaps. Yes. Roses would suit her now. A cake with white icing and red roses to mark the day.

Then, glancing once more at Sophie, Jenny quickly dismisses the thought.

On the television, the face of Arthur Scargill fills the screen, with his wiry, brillo-pad hair and his tiny, angry eyes. Simon hits the volume control and defiant talk about *pits* and *strikes* and *closures* fills the room. Outside the colliery gates, picketers shout and jostle with police as Jenny looks on, wondering where all this will lead to and how it will end.

*

In the night, Jenny hears the squeak of the floor-boards on the landing at the top of the stairs and the click of the catch as the door to Charlotte's bedroom is pushed open and pulled closed. She is home now. *Safe.* And Jenny is able to breathe. Staring up into the darkness, she feels Simon shift next to her then settle again. How does he manage to sleep, she wonders, when so much is at stake?

Jenny closes her eyes, but the thought of Charlotte just down the hall nags at her. She should get out of bed and talk to her. Right now. Before it's too late. But would Charlotte even listen to what she has to say? Lately, it seems, they can barely be in the same room without Charlotte taking offence. And she can't remember the last time they talked. Really talked. Just the two of them. Together. It's Simon that Charlotte goes to, now. She listens to him. She confides in him. She doesn't need a mother any more. But there are things Jenny could tell their daughter that Simon can't. Things only a woman would know.

She should get out of bed and go to Charlotte's room. Right now. She has to tell her that better things await than Ian. Better men are out there. There's no need to rush. And these blasted A-levels, they'll be good, don't worry. Everything is going to be just fine. And more than anything else, she needs to tell her daughter that she loves her. Much more than she can find the words to say. She should get up right now and go to Charlotte's room and tell her all the things she needs her to know while there's still time.

But the weight of the darkness is impossibly heavy, pressing against her chest and wrapping around her legs, and dragging her down into another night of unsettled sleep.

*

At the start of her shift, Jenny makes her way to Taylor's desk at the end of the middle row of back-to-back letter frames and joins the queue to sign in. If he leans to his right Taylor can look down the aisle between two of the rows, surveying nearly half of the shift of mail sorters without leaving his chair, and if he leans to his left, another twenty workers come into view. Should he choose to hoist himself from his throne and walk to the end of the fifth row of frames, the rest of the shift would fall under his gaze. Three rows of letter frames and two rows of flats. Fifty mail sorters when all the frames are full. That's quite a little kingdom.

'What do you fancy today, kid?' Roger rubs his hands together and feigns an expression of glee as Jenny signs the register. 'Letters or flats? I can do you a nice assortment of magazines and catalogues. Might even throw in a few thousand A4 envelopes. First class, if you're lucky.'

Taylor cuts in before she can answer with a suitable quip. 'Letters. Both of you.'

Jenny passes the pen to Roger. 'Thank goodness for small favours. I hate sorting flats.'

Taylor leans back in his chair and folds his arms. 'Don't get too comfortable. There's another delivery due later this morning. You'll have plenty of flats to sort then.'

Jenny grins at Taylor through gritted teeth. 'Sorry, did I say I *hate* flats? I meant to say I *love* them. Honestly, they're absolutely the best.'

'Go on,' he barks. 'Get to work and stop wasting time.'

Roger clicks his heels together and offers a stiff salute. 'Aye, aye, sir. And you have a lovely day, too.' Turning sharply, he leads Jenny towards two vacant frames at the far end of the row.

*

It is a typical beach scene: blue sky, white sand, leaning palms. One of the perks of sorting mail is looking at postcards from other people's holidays. Jenny glances at the card, then lays it picture side up on the bench where her mind can wander through it as she works. Postcards from beach holidays, though, are meagre inspiration and she longs for a more engaging view to come along: sunrise behind the pyramids on the Giza Plateau, Icelandic geysers shooting skywards, a mule train picking its way down the side of the Grand Canyon. Her favourite card so far this summer has been from a girl who called herself Miracle. The picture was of a sand-coloured temple surrounded by shorn-headed boys in saffron robes, and Miracle, so she wrote, had found *tranquillity*.

When her bench is clear again, Jenny upends a fresh box of letters and spreads its contents in front of the wooden frame. She grabs a handful of the envelopes, and clutching them close to her chest she begins sorting once more. Her right hand plucks crisp endearments and Telecom bills from her left, and casts them into pigeonholes marked Preston and Leeds and Plymouth and York in smooth, sharp, continuous strokes. Two minutes for each clutch of letters. Twenty for each box. Fifteen hundred letters an hour.

It takes her fifteen minutes to cycle to work each morning, and another five to weave her way past the receiving and dispatch bays in the cavernous hall beneath the building before climbing the steps to the sorting room. For five years, she has been the only woman to stick with the job, and the only woman in the building outside of the canteen and the offices upstairs. Swiftly, she works her way through each box of letters, the local pigeonholes filling up fast: Milton, Hilsea, Southsea, Cosham. On occasion, there are still catcalls from the men, but she has grown used to their banter and deaf to their jibes.

The sorting room is vast – the size of a small city block with an equally large population: men sorting packets and parcels and bulk mail and letters; men running machines; men dividing the post into neighbourhoods and streets, ready for local delivery;

men pushing York trolleys around the floor; men laughing; men shouting. On the north and west sides of the sorting room, two floors of offices rise above the main hall, their blackened windows overlooking the machines and the men and her. In all the time Jenny has worked in the sorting room, she has been upstairs only once. The day she was interviewed, tested, hired and trained. As she works, she glances up at the windows from time to time and wonders if someone is behind the glass looking down.

At the next frame, Roger works steadily, his gaze unwavering as though he's in a trance. There are sixty-four pigeonholes in his letter frame, and he knows the exact position of each one by heart. Jenny watches him out of the corner of her eye. His hands barely move as letters fly, one after another, towards their final destinations.

Behind the row of letter frames at her back, the CFC – a machine as big as a house – drones through the day as it tumbles letters into place, turning them face out and cancelling their stamps, before they are boxed and stacked and pushed into a line of York trolleys, ready to be sorted by hand. Until the end of the late shift, when the machines are switched off and the letter frames are cleared, the sorting office is never still. Fans whir overhead. Machinery rumbles and clatters. Yorks clunk together as they are wheeled into their rows. Somewhere nearby, a transistor is tuned to Radio 2, but the music is drowned out by the noise.

When she has finished the last of the letters on her bench Jenny picks up the beach postcard she had set to one side earlier in the morning, ready to toss it into her frame with the rest. Turning it over to check its destination, she finds the words 'insufficient address' scrawled in the white space next to 'Isle of Wight'. The name of the town and the postcode are missing. Its only destination now is the Dead Letter Office at the far end of the sorting-room floor.

She scans the message quickly.

Life is nothing without you in it.

'Right there, Jennifer.' Taylor's voice looms up suddenly from behind and causes her to jump.

She flings the postcard into the dead-letter box and turns to see him, hands on hips, rocking on the balls of his feet. His tie is pulled loose and off-centre at his neck and the tip of it overhangs the great mound of his belly.

'Time for your test,' he says, adding a sharp clap of his hands.

'But... but you tested me last month.' She glances at Roger.

'That's right,' Roger said. 'You did. And you haven't tested me in years.'

'Too late for old buggers like you. Besides, you're out of this place before long. No point.' Taylor turns again to Jenny. 'The man upstairs says your speed and accuracy need be checked. It's nothing personal. Clear down your frame and get your letters laid out on the bench.' Taylor reaches past Jenny and begins pulling envelopes from her frame, securing each bundle with an elastic band and dropping it into a box.

'Strange how my turn comes round so fast,' she mumbles.

'Why are you females always so touchy?' Taylor snaps. 'I'm just doing what I'm told. And you, my dear, should learn to do the same. There are plenty of men in the dole queues who could take your place tomorrow. It wouldn't hurt you to remember that.'

Jenny pulls the postcard from the dead-letter box before it disappears into a bundle, and slides it on to the corner of Roger's bench when Taylor's back is turned.

'Bastard,' she says under her breath, then empties a box of fresh letters on her bench.

Roger leans towards her. 'Don't worry about him. You're one of the best letter sorters he has. You got this.'

'All right, Jennifer.' Taylor studies his watch. 'You know the drill. Okay, now start.'

Clutching a handful of letters in her left hand, she begins feeding the envelopes into the frame. DE21 – Derby – top left. PO19 – Chichester – second box from bottom, third from the right. BS1 – Bristol – far right, two boxes down from the top. As she gets into her stride, letters flow from hand to frame as if she is dealing cards for a game of rummy. She reads the postcodes with fluency, barely glancing at the frame as she flings the envelopes into their little compartments. After all this time, it feels instinctive now, like breathing. She doesn't have to think, doesn't have to process. All she needs to do is read the postcode and toss the letter into the right box. It's as easy as that.

She glances over her shoulder and raises an eyebrow at Roger. He has slowed his pace, keeping half an eye on Taylor and half on her. 'How am I doing?'

He gives her the thumbs-up. 'Keep concentrating, kid. No showing off.'

She rolls her eyes then pauses to look at an address.

'Newport,' she says, looking directly at Roger. 'There are eight bloody Newports in the country and this idiot can't be bothered to tell us which one he's writing to.'

'Just drop it on the bench and keep going, Jen.'

The handwritten envelope has a Portsmouth address in the corner, so she takes a chance. She taps it against the bench and tosses it into the box bound for the Isle of Wight.

'You're almost there, kid. Keep it up!'

Jenny senses Taylor standing behind her and imagines him drumming his fingers on his stomach as he counts down the final seconds. He's standing so close she can almost feel his breath on her neck. The thought of him there makes her skin crawl but she refuses to let him distract her. She's good at this. She knows she is, and she won't be intimidated.

'Right. That's it. Go for a break while we see how you did.'

Roger drops his fist of letters on his bench. 'She did great. You know she did. She always does.'

He follows Jenny as she heads to the lift and the canteen upstairs. 'Have you heard about that new woman round the corner, on flats?' He waits for the lift doors to close before he continues. 'Old Stalin has been pushing his weight around. He pulled her into the office, yesterday. Said she needed to buck up or she'd be out the door.'

Jenny shakes her head. 'Taylor doesn't like having women on his patch. She needs to go to the union or he'll end up forcing her out like he's done the others.'

*

The card has remained on her bench since she retrieved it from Roger, and throughout the day she has picked it up a dozen times and gazed at the glossy picture on the front. A white sand beach separating an azure sea from an azure sky. Palm trees. A wooden hut in the corner, and an empty beach chair opened out before it as if waiting for someone to sit down and relax.

'Clear down!'

Taylor's voice bellows along the row of frames, signalling the end of the shift. Arms folded across his chest, he stands at the end of the row watching the mail sorters begin to empty the frames.

Jenny is reliable, accurate and fast. She knows Taylor can't fault her work. And he can't sack her just because she's a woman. He would need a legitimate reason. The thought of Roger retiring to Australia leaves her feeling sick and desperate. He has been her one true ally since she's been at this job, and once he's gone she'll have to battle with Taylor on her own. She glances back along the queue of mail sorters as they file past the frames, grabbing envelopes from the pigeonholes and bundling them up. She scans the blackened security windows that rise above the sorting office floor and wonders if someone is up there now, watching her. The line of frames is being cleared; one by one, the pigeonholes are emptied. As she adds the postcard to the clutch of letters from the dead-letter box, ready to be banded up, someone bumps her elbow and the letters fall to the floor.

'Sorry, love,' a voice calls out, as the line of men trundles past.

Bending now, she sees the postcard face up in the aisle and snatches it to safety before it is stepped on. Feet shuffle around her as she hunches over the fallen letters. Quickly, Jenny gathers them to her then looks at the card one last time before pushing it up her sleeve.

Deborah,
I've been stumbling around out here unable to think of anything but you. I was stupid to walk out like that, and now I'm half a world away and worried I've lost you forever. Please forgive me.

Life is nothing without you in it. I'll be at my sister's until the end of August. If I don't hear from you by then, I'll know it's really over. Please phone.
  Michael

*

Jenny turns the taps and sits on the edge of the bath, looking at the card in her hands. Taking it had been a stupid thing to do. A sackable offence. *What on earth was she thinking?* Three million people were already out of work, and every day the dole queues grew longer. Jobs, decent jobs, were impossible to find. And now, just like that she's gone and thrown hers away. *What had possessed her to do it?* Monday afternoon, at the start of her shift, they'll call her into the office. Someone must have seen her. If not someone watching from the security windows up above, then someone on the floor – someone wanting to score brownie points with the management. Someone who needed a legitimate reason to get rid of her. And that would be it. A good job down the pan. And for what? Some lovelorn boy who can't even remember his girlfriend's address.

She studies the stamps in the corner of the card. An eighteen-cent rainbow lorikeet and a thirty-cent kangaroo. They add an exotic feel to the photograph on the front. The card itself is like a hundred others that have passed through her hands – a cliché of a beach scene – but the stamps are extraordinary!

Lifting the postcard to her face, she tries to breathe in the perfumed air of the rainforest – sweet and thick and humid – but all she can smell are the Superdrug bath crystals dissolving in the tub of water.

She remembers now all the cards and letters that fell through their letter box after Aunt Kate emigrated to Australia, and the string-bound parcels that arrived in time for Christmas – posted in the Antipodean spring and filled with the scent of perpetual summer. She'd been eight years old when this strange other world revealed itself, and by studying the map on the schoolroom wall she had discovered that the seas were all connected. Two years later, after her father left home, Aunt Kate began adding a pinch of sand to every letter she posted as a temptation to Jenny's mother to cross the world and start again. Once or twice her mother had seemed ready to make the move, but something always held her back, and in the end they never ventured further than Butlin's at Bognor. The sea in Sussex, her mother claimed, was every bit as good as the sea that lapped the beaches of Melbourne. 'And our fish won't chew your leg off while you're drowning.'

Jenny had saved the precious grains of sand in an empty Colman's mustard jar and when she left home and married Simon she had taken the jar with her. Now and then, when she feels herself disappearing into his or Charlotte's life, a minor character in their stories, she holds the jar to the window and watches the light glinting off the tiny crystals, dreaming of the life she could have had, somewhere warm and far away.

The postmark on the card reads *Coolangatta, 20 July 1984*. In three weeks, it has travelled the world and the Isle of Wight. Now, though, it is just another dead letter. She studies the address: Deborah Cunningham, 7 Edward Cottages, Isle of Wight, England. Room had been left for the street name and the town, but Michael had absent-mindedly posted the card without double-checking the address. What was it, Jenny wonders, that had caused the rift? Had he been as careless in his affections as he was in his correspondence? Whatever the transgression, the poor boy now seemed genuinely sorry. Surely he was worthy of another chance.

Lying back in the bath, Jenny reads the message again. The couple would be in their early twenties, she decides: young enough to be traumatised by love, but old enough, *hopefully*, not to be destroyed by it. She remembers the depths of youthful passions – the physical pain of heartbreak – and the unbelievable joy of loving and being loved again. But then – somewhere along the way things changed. The highs and lows were gone, and the desperate sense of love and anguish and turmoil was transformed into an agreeable stability before sweeping headlong into indifference. She knows that Simon's mouth will never again form the words that Michael has written: *Life is nothing without you*. Letting the postcard drop to the floor, she sinks beneath the water.

Once, long ago, she'd had the opportunity for something different. But like her mother, she'd turned her back on the life that could have been and let it walk away. If only she'd been braver and taken the chance, who knew where she might be right now and who she might have become. She thinks of those grains of Australian sand, that empty beach and Michael's mournful plea. What has happened to her life? Where has it gone? When did she get so *old*?

'Shit, shit, shit,' she mutters out loud as she surfaces.

At the door there is an urgent knock. 'Jenny, is that you in there?'

She had not announced her arrival when she returned from work, but instead had gone straight up the stairs to run a bath. Now, though, Simon has found her.

'Yes. Sorry,' she calls back, then winces at her own words. She apologises instinctively these days.

'I've eaten without you. Charlotte's gone to the pictures with Ian.'

She takes a deep breath and tries to remember what life was like before Ian came into it.

'Jen?'

'Yeah. That's okay. I'm not hungry.'

Simon is silent, but she knows he is still there on the other side of the door, waiting, just as she waits. Listening. She imagines his hand on the door knob and wonders if he will try to come in. When their marriage was still new, she never felt the need to lock it, and sometimes he would sit on the bathroom floor as she bathed and the two of them would talk about all the minutes and hours they'd spent apart. But after nearly twenty years together, it is as if their quota of words is almost gone and they have to ration them out, sparingly, in case they one day have something important to say to each other again. Still, she senses he is waiting for her to say something now, as though he is waiting for a reply to a question asked long ago. She wishes she could offer him one but there are no words to chase away the silence that hangs between them. She wants to shout. She wants to scream. How did things wind up this way? He deserves an answer, but she has none and remains silent.

Finally, she hears the creak of the floor beneath his feet as he walks away. She closes her eyes as his footsteps retreat down the stairs and lets her body slide deeper into the bath until she is all but suspended, ears and eyes below the waterline, listening to the sounds of her breath and her heartbeat. Five beats for every intake of air. Five beats for every exhalation. If all the seas and all the currents and all the tides are bound together, constantly journeying from one corner of the world to another, how long would it take for a lilo, swept out to sea, to drift all the way to Australia?

*

She tucks the postcard between the centre pages of a copy of *Woman's Own* and places the magazine beneath the bed. Taking it had been a rash and sentimental act. No good could possibly come of it. Tomorrow, she'll drop it in the postbox on the corner and let it join the other letters with incomplete or illegible addresses so that someone in the Dead Letter Office can find where it belongs. That's what they do. That's what they get paid for. They track people down and give them year-old get-well cards and birthday greetings from deceased grandmothers with pound notes pinned inside. She's heard stories about Mrs Smith of 110 London Road or Mr C. Davies from somewhere in Cardiff receiving these resurrected letters, and she pictures a team of weary posties cycling up and down the country, unable to rest until they've located the right address. *Unbelievable!* She knows of posties who can trace council tenants when they move house without telling the gas board, trawling through telephone directories and electoral rolls to reunite old ladies with their unpaid bills, but she hasn't met one who'd spend an ounce of energy on a postcard with only half an address written by a heartbroken boy in Australia. Michael's card truly was a dead letter. And there was nothing she could do about it.

But the message pulls her back. Retrieving the magazine, she flicks through its pages until she finds the postcard, then turns it over to look at its lost words – *Life is nothing without you in it* – and remembers a boy she once knew. *Paolo*. He had been her one real chance for romance and adventure. Before life got in the way.

*

Jenny listens a while to the steady rhythm of Simon's breathing, then rolls on to her side and sees his profile silhouetted against the glow of early morning light that filters through the bedroom window. Sleep is deceptive, she thinks. It makes him look at ease with the world. When she watches him like this, without his knowing, when he is unguarded and free of worry, she is certain that everything between them will be okay. That enough of their old life still exists, that they can take what's left and use it to create something new to sustain them into the future. Despite their problems, Simon is a good man, still. A *steady man*, her mother once called him. A man who would never abandon his family as Jenny's own father did. She should be thankful for that. Watching him now, Jenny remembers Simon as he was. Confident, in his shy, awkward sort of way. Easily content and happy with his lot. What happened, she wonders. *To him? To us? To me?* In the quiet of the early morning, tenderness returns and she thinks of him as another lost child, one she still hopes will find his way home.

She reaches beneath the duvet and rests a hand on his stomach. His breathing grows deeper and he moves towards her without opening his eyes. For years, she half-waited for him to grow bored with her and run off with someone else. But he never did. He is faithful. He is steady. And she knows he is not the one who would ever choose to leave. She had wasted so much time being afraid of things that never happened when the thing she should have feared the most crept up on her, unnoticed. And now it's there between them, growing stronger and pushing her away.

Slipping out of bed, she leaves Simon to his dreams and crosses the hall to her daughters' room. Cautiously, she pushes the door open and peers into the pinkish, pre-dawn light. Mounds of clothing litter the floor around Charlotte's bed, carelessly dropped and kicked aside, and straying into Sophie's half of the room. The disarray annoys Jenny, but when her eyes rest upon the lone figure beneath the duvet she lets the feeling pass. Charlotte, at least, is safe. Against the opposite wall, Sophie's bed remains as tidy as a display in a department store window, a regiment of teddy bears keeping chaos at bay.

She carries the *Woman's Own* downstairs, careful not to bend the card hidden within its pages. In the kitchen, she checks the calendar. Sunday. The twelfth of August. It is two weeks until Michael's end-of-the-month deadline. On the back of a discarded envelope she writes *Gone to do overtime*, and leaves the note propped against the jar of

Nescafé on the kitchen table. She checks her watch as she wheels her bicycle out of the shed. It has just gone six o'clock. She has just enough time to catch the 6.20 ferry to Ryde.

But there's no time to waste.

II

The sun hangs at the edge of the pale morning sky as the ferry approaches the island. Jenny tries to read what the day has in store from the feathery clouds that streak the sky above her. The morning, at least, will be dry and clear. From the seafront in Southsea, her eyes have skimmed across the Solent to trace the outline of the island a thousand times. At that distance she could see most of the north side, a thin body of land, hugging the sea like a surfboard – or a lilo – rising in the east with the chalk hills of Culver Down and slipping away towards the Needles in the west. But as the ferry draws alongside Ryde Pier, the island stretches out, the east and west of it disappearing into the distance. All of a sudden the island has become massive. Following the line of Ryde town from the shoreline to the thrusting bell tower of All Saints, she tries to stay positive. Though she can no longer see its entirety in one glance, the island is not really as big as it now seems. One hundred and fifty square miles according to her map. That's all.

On a bench on the Esplanade, she pulls her tartan flask from the basket on the front of her bike and pours herself a cup of milky tea. She needs to think. She needs to make a plan.

With the Ordnance Survey map spread wide on the ground at her feet, she traces the A3055 as it circles the island, becoming the A3054 at Totland – sixty-five, maybe seventy-five miles around. Apart from Newport, the biggest towns lie alongside the coast. More than likely Deborah Cunningham lives in one of these. Jenny starts to relax as a plan takes shape. She will work her way round the edge of the island before heading inland. That makes sense. Ryde, Cowes and then Newport. The villages in the interior of the island can be ignored for the time being. She has plenty of time: all of today, next weekend, and the long bank holiday at the end of the month. With a bit of luck, she'll find Deborah long before the time expires.

'Right,' she says aloud, spotting a phone box down the street. 'Let's try doing things the easy way.'

Thumbing through the directory, she locates three people in Ryde by the name of Cunningham, none of them with the address of 7 Edward Cottages. She is neither surprised nor deterred, though, and scrawls the numbers on the back of the *Woman's Own*.

It is Sunday morning and she stands astride her bicycle listening to the silence that surrounds her. She likes this time of day best of all, when the rest of the world hasn't yet woken up, and a sense of peace hangs in the air. The streets are empty. No cars passing by; no music spilling from the penny arcade opposite the pier; no shrieks from children playing on the beach beneath the Esplanade. Just silence. Then, from behind her comes the hum of movement, barely a whisper between the houses. As she turns to search for the sound, a milk float glides past the end of the street.

Pushing off from the kerb, she gives chase.

She races after it as far as Eastern Gardens, then turns up Dover Street where the road rises sharply up the hill. Instantly, the bike slows into the climb. Cycling in Portsmouth does not involve hills and she cannot remember the last time she has needed to change gear. Struggling on, she wills the pedals to turn. Finally, the bicycle stops moving forward altogether and she watches the milk float pull away.

Pushing the bike now, she jogs as fast as she can up the hill, but the distance between her and the milk float continues to widen. Finally, gasping for breath, she has to stop. Clinging to her bicycle she cries out as loud as she can, 'Wait!'

Embarrassed by the sound of her voice in the still, sleepy hours of the morning she glances around at the houses lining the street. Old women will be peeking through their net curtains to see what's going on. But she can't let this opportunity pass. At the top of the hill, the milk float pulls to the side of the road to make a delivery, and the milkman, in his white smock coat and cap steps into the open.

'Excuse me,' she calls out again. Her voice is lower this time with an added measure of restraint, and the man continues about his business without looking up. Grasping two pint bottles from a crate on the back of his float, he proceeds to the gate at the front of a house and disappears behind a hedge. Jenny presses on, jogging up the hill again, determined to catch him before he slips away, and she is waiting for him when he emerges from the garden. 'G'morning,' she says, trying to steady her breath.

The milkman looks startled at first, then breaks into a ready smile. 'You about give me a fright, young lady. Thought you might've been one of them highway bandits after a pint of my gold top.'

He waits for her to catch her breath. 'Them hills'll get you if you aren't careful. They're not so big but they're plenty steep.'

Jenny returns the milkman's smile. 'I'm trying to find an address, and you look like you might know your way around the neighbourhood.' Though she has memorised every word, she retrieves the postcard from her basket and reads the address out loud.

The milkman sucks air through his teeth as he drops the two empty milk bottles he has collected into a crate. 'Number seven Edward Cottages, eh?' He gazes into the distance as if he's searching a street map in his head, then purses his lips. 'Sorry, love. Can't say I've heard of it.' But he directs her up the road and round the corner – right, then left, then right again to Edward Street. 'Could be something tucked away there, I suppose.'

She pedals away, waving a trail of thanks behind her.

The search has begun.

*

There are no Edward Cottages on Edward Street, however, and neither the paperboy she passes nor the man at the newsagent's is able to help. She wonders how often she will need to ask for help along the way. Local knowledge will be essential if she's to stand a chance of finding Deborah. Twice should be enough for villages with fewer than two public houses, she decides, and six times for larger towns or those with new estates. That sounds reasonable.

From the top of the high street she looks out across the water to Portsmouth. Sunlight glints off windows and rooftops now and shimmers like silver fish along the shoreline. Her own front door is little more than five miles from where she stands, but the narrow strip of water between the city and the island makes home feel like a distant world to her now, and the island where she stands feels somehow foreign and unknown. She glances at her watch. Nobody at home will have noticed her absence yet. Simon and Charlotte will still be asleep. And when they wake? How long, she wonders, would she have to stay away before they realised she was gone?

She carries on up Swanmore then follows Upton Road, climbing away from the silver-blue line of the sea. It is a steep climb on her heavy five-speed roadster but this time she remembers to shift down a gear and she is surprised when the wheels continue to turn. It's years since she's been so far from home without Simon or the girls directing her way, and being without them now feels like she is charting unclaimed territory.

At the junction at the top of the hill, she stops. A patchwork of fields, golden, green and muddy brown, spreads out below, each square stitched on to the next with a hem of hawthorn and bramble. From here, she has the choice of four roads: three going forward, one going back. The decision of which to take is hers, and hers alone. And the feeling of anticipation is delicious. She lifts her chin and breathes in the tangy-sweet scents of newly mown hay, leaf-mould and manure, then places her foot on the pedal, eyes the road to her right, and pushes off with conviction. As the road curves away, Portsmouth winks out of sight.

The road drops all the way into Havenstreet, and the wind created as she speeds along it whips through her hair. This must be what it's like to fly, she thinks, and she is halfway through the village before she remembers to stop.

*

'What can I get for you today?'

There was a sandwich and a nearly full flask of tea in her basket, but the café on the edge of Newport town centre, with its red gingham curtains was too inviting to pass by. *Nan's*, read the sign in the window, *Just Like Home*. She'd been looking for a park with a bench where she could stop to eat her lunch, but when she reached the quiet high street and saw the posy of flowers on the table in the café window she decided the sandwich would keep. If the afternoon was anything like the morning, she'd need the extra energy to get home. According to her map, she was little more than ten miles from the end of Ryde Pier, but according to her watch, half the day was already gone. She'd lost track of the number of hills she'd been forced to climb on foot, and the times she'd turned left instead of right and wound up lost or going in circles. Still, the time hadn't been wasted. She'd looked for Edward Cottages along every road and every lane. Sometimes twice.

The young girl waiting tables looks no more than thirteen or fourteen but she's good at making small talk and putting the Sunday customers at their ease. As she hovers by the table waiting for Jenny's order, she gives no indication of the moodiness that infected her own girls at that age. She's cheerful and confident. The owner's daughter, maybe. Or granddaughter.

Jenny orders egg and chips and 'a big pot of tea', then turns her attention back to the scene outside the window. A thin stream of people has begun to filter through the doors of the minster just down the street, and she follows them as they disappear down side streets and pass the front of the café: old women on their own or in pairs going home to their empty houses, young mothers with children in tow. Behind her, a bell jangles as the café door is pushed open. After a pause and a brief, whispered conversation two elderly women sit down at the next table. Jenny glances up from the window as they scoot their chairs into position and the women nod their greeting. On the street outside, a cluster of young tourists, one of them holding a map at arm's length so the others can see, stand on the corner. The boys wear dark trousers and neat, button-down shirts; the girls, knee-length summer dresses and little flat shoes. Smart but practical. They are students, maybe. Possibly foreign. Having an adventure before summer ends. One of the girls draws her finger along the map, then points behind them to something out of sight, and they all turn in unison to look. They laugh as the map is refolded and put away, and continue down the street.

'Off to the villa, I expect.' Jenny glances at the women at the next table and catches the eye of the one who spoke. They, too, have been watching the group of young people gathered on the corner.

'The Roman villa?' the woman says to Jenny. 'Have you been?'

Just then, the young waitress returns with a pot of tea.

'There you go,' she says. 'I'll be right back with your lunch.' As she turns back to the kitchen she glances at the two women. 'You all right there, Mrs B? Mrs M?'

A moment later she returns with Jenny's lunch. 'Is there anything else I can get for you? Any ketchup? Or brown sauce?'

Jenny shakes her head. 'No. That's fine. Thank you.'

When the waitress has gone, she slips Michael's card from the magazine and places it against the little vase of flowers on her table. She lifts the lid on the teapot and gives it a stir before pouring the tea into her cup, then adding the milk and a spoonful of sugar. She looks again at the beach and the little shack in the distance as she stirs her tea. For the first time since setting out that morning she questions what she's really doing. Does she honestly think she can find Deborah by riding her bicycle around the island, aimlessly, looking for her address? She might as well stand on the steps of the guildhall calling out her name. If she had any sense at all, she'd deposit the blasted card in the nearest postbox and catch the next ferry home. She could make a nice tea for Simon and Charlotte, something that didn't come out of a packet or a plastic bag for a change, go back to work tomorrow afternoon, talk nicely to Taylor, pretend that none of this ever happened and carry on as usual. That's what she should do. *What is the point, after all?*

Some young couple had an argument. So what? It's nothing to do with her. It's none of her business. They'll either sort themselves out or they won't, just like everybody else. One way or another, the world will keep turning just the same.

She used to be curious about the people who sat alone in pubs and cafés, wondering if they were lonely and wanted company; if they were friendless by choice or irritable and irksome by nature and good at driving people away. But now she sees that there's a freedom in being unknown and alone, with time to think unhindered by conversation and other people's thoughts. She can sit here as long as she likes, eating as slowly as she likes. No one is going to start drumming their fingers on the tablecloth, urging her to hurry up.

When Jenny has finished her lunch, she picks up the postcard and turns it over to look at the back again. Each time she reads the words she feels the desperation once more.

'Would you like more tea?' The girl has returned to clear away the empty plates.

Jenny shakes her head. 'No. I'm just about finished, thanks.'

She nods at the postcard in Jenny's hand. 'Looks like somebody's been on holiday. That's nowhere around here, for sure.'

Jenny holds the card up so the girl can look at the picture. 'Australia,' she says. 'Somewhere called Coolangatta.'

The girl sighs. 'It looks dreamy, doesn't it?'

Jenny looks at the name badge on the girl's blouse. 'Lily, is it?' She might as well ask for help while she's here. 'I'm trying to find a woman named Deborah Cunningham. This card belongs to her, but I only have part of her address.' Jenny hands the postcard to the girl so she can read the message on the back. 'I need to make sure she gets it.'

Lily admires the tropical beach for a moment, then turns the card over to look at the back. 'Pretty stamps,' she says.

Her eyes pass slowly over the message before moving on to the address.

'Oh!' she says, looking at Jenny again. 'And you're trying to find Deborah so they can get back together?' Instinctively, she seems to understand.

'That's what I was hoping to do, but it doesn't seem likely, does it? I don't have much to go on.'

Lily bites her lower lip. 'No. I guess you don't. But isn't that the fun of a good mystery? Looking for the clues?' She looks at the address again. 'Gosh! Deborah's whole future depends on you. You have to at least try to find her.' Her eyes are bright and wide.

Jenny smiles. Lily is right. She's only just started looking. She can't give up now.

'I know!' the girl says, her eyes wide with possibilities. 'I'll ask my nan. She owns this café and knows absolutely everyone. I can ask the customers, too.'

Without pausing, she turns to the two old women at the table next to Jenny's. 'Have you heard of Edward Cottages? Do you know anyone named Deborah Cunningham?'

The women shake their heads, but Lily's enthusiasm rekindles Jenny's belief in her mission. Deborah and Michael need her as nobody else needs her right now. Once the card is delivered, they'll be free to go forward in whatever direction they choose. Without it, though, their choices have been denied. She can't simply ignore their plight. She must do what she can to help.

*

As she rides north out of Newport, the walls of Parkhurst Prison flash through the gaps in the hedge alongside the road. It is mid-afternoon and the traffic is light, but she keeps her eyes focused on the tarmac as the road begins to climb again. The climb is long and steep and she thumbs the shifter down a notch, then down again as the wheels lose momentum, rolling slower with each push of the pedals. She shifts into her lowest gear and wills herself forward, on to the next tarred crack in the road, the next fence post and tree and telephone pole. A car beeps as it over-takes her, passing closer and faster than it should. She lifts her head to watch it pull away and seeks the top of the hill. It looks no nearer than when she began this climb and the sight of it, still so far away,

crushes the last of her strength. The bic[y]... [s]
as it slows even more and she puts her ...
before she loses her balance entirely and ...
the ground. She can go no further, and stan...
side of the road, shaking. Why does everythi...
to be so bloody hard?

In the past two years she and Simon have w...
out a new routine for themselves and they ...
become so well practised at appearing content t...
she sometimes believes it herself. Throughout the d...
they move smoothly in overlapping circles, glidin...
round one another in movements precisely tuned
to avoid collision. They have never been dramatic
in their disagreements and in all the years they've
been together, they've never descended into shouting
or had a full-blown row. He's never lifted his hand
against her. She's never slammed a door. Simon is a
good man. A faithful husband. A loving father to
Charlotte. To an outsider, their marriage is as solid as
the walls of Parkhurst Prison. A happy couple *despite
their misfortune*. Made stronger because of it. But
the intimacy they shared in that other life is gone; the
fearless words, honestly spoken, now remain unsaid.
Part of her still longs to share his life, his dreams, his
thoughts. Part of her just wants to flee.

At Northwood, she turns towards Gurnard before
swooping back along the Solent again into Cowes.
On the seafront, she stops an ambling dog walker
to enquire about Edward Cottages and on the ferry
across the Medina she asks again. Twice more she

43

ops as she climbs her way through Whippingham
nd on up to Wootton Bridge. Each shake of the
ead is a new defeat. But it's only the first day, she
reminds herself, as she returns to the ferry at Ryde.
There is plenty of time to find Deborah before the
end of the month.

III

Jenny feels Taylor watching her as she carries the box of letters past his desk to her frame at the far end of the line. As she begins feeding envelopes into the pigeonholes she imagines his eyes still upon her, and each time she looks down the row, there he is, watching. Each time she catches his eye, she turns away, shifts uneasily, pretends to stretch or look for Roger, but she knows Taylor is not fooled. He watches her purposely. Someone saw her take the card and now he's just waiting for his moment to pounce. Soon, she'll be marched into one of the offices upstairs for questioning. By the end of the night, she'll be out of a job.

One after another, letters fly from her fingers with machine-like accuracy: Norwich, Birmingham, Fareham, Perth; Glasgow, Newcastle, London, York; Plymouth, Winchester, Hayling, Crewe; Reading, Scarborough, Bognor, Bude. As the envelopes click against the back of the boxes she escapes into the rhythm of the work and thinks again of Deborah and Michael, remembering how it felt to be young and in love.

His name was Paolo. No. His name was actually Paul – just an ordinary name for an ordinary boy from an ordinary street in North End. But he wanted to *reinvent* himself, he had told her, and begin his life again. Jenny had thought him daring and exotic, and she liked the breathy feel of his name in her mouth, the way it flicked across her tongue and shaped her lips into a perfectly kissable pout: *Pow-lo*.

Her mother, though, disliked him from the start.

'You better watch yourself with that one,' she had said after the only occasion when Jenny had brought him home for tea. 'He doesn't want you for your money is all I can say.' After her father left, *with that tart of his*, Jenny's mother had become an authority on men. And most of them, in her opinion, weren't to be trusted.

When Paolo dropped out of art college to travel the world, he had begged her to go with him. The continent was only a train ride and a ferry ticket away. Paris, Amsterdam, Venice, Rome. It was all right there. So close.

But when she faltered at the first step, he had left without her.

Cambridge, Exeter, Cardiff, Hove; Bournemouth, Sunderland, Brighton, Knowle.

His final letter arrived the day Simon asked her to marry him. 'Life means nothing without you in it.'

*

'So, you think you can get away from me by hiding down here?'

Startled, Jenny drops a handful of letters on the bench.

'Bloody hell, Roger.' She quickly reclaims the envelopes and turns them face up in her hand, the letter to Knowle on top. Without glancing at Roger, she peels the letter off the stack, then grimaces.

'Bit jumpy today, kid.' Roger peers at the letter in her hand and spots the missing postcode. 'What you got there?' He plucks the envelope from her fingers and studies the address. 'There's a Knowle down in Devon. And another near Bristol. And one more in the West Midlands. But I expect it's the one here in Hampshire, don't you?' He turns to his own frame and flicks the letter into the pigeonhole for PO17. 'There. Problem solved. Now, what else is bothering you? Simon? Taylor?'

Jenny shrugs her shoulders and begins feeding letters into her frame again, slower this time.

'Listen, if it's Taylor, you need to forget about him.' Roger empties a box of letters on his bench. 'He's just a bully-boy. These ex-navy types like to push their weight around. Makes them feel good. But it's all bluff and beans. There's more of us than there is of them. That's what you have to remember. There's strength in numbers. You coming to the union meeting tomorrow?'

Jenny nods. 'I'll be there. Gotta stand together and all that, haven't we?'

'That's right, especially once things start heating up around here.'

She stops and looks at Roger. 'What have you heard?'

He taps the side of his nose. 'You'll find out tomorrow.'

*

Jenny sniffs the air as she enters the house – cigarette smoke – and knows immediately that Ian is there. She finds him in the sitting room, perched on the sofa with Simon. Just like a couple of bookends, she thinks. Neither of them looks up as she peers round the door. She watches them leaning towards the telly as if something momentous were about to be revealed, then glances at the television screen. *Cricket.*

'Would anyone else like a cup of tea?' She opens the door wide and enters the room.

Simon raises the flat of his hand. 'Shh, Botham's about to bowl.'

For months now, Jenny has felt herself grow thinner, as if the molecules that make up her body were disassembling themselves and she was gradually vanishing into the ether. She fears that the most substantial part of her now is her breath and wonders how long it will be before she completely disappears.

And will it even matter when she does?

The silence in the room is punctuated by the sharp thwack of ball meeting bat, then resumes as the camera follows the ball through the sky. Simon and Ian lean further into the television, eyes fixed and breath held.

Ian is the first to break the silence. 'Ahh!' he moans as the ball hits the ground and rolls along the grass. He flops back into the cushions, scattering cigarette ash across her sofa. 'Did you see that? Even I could have caught that ball.'

Jenny waits at the door a moment longer, but neither man looks her way. Backing out of the room, she pulls the door closed behind her.

Upstairs, beside the bed she sees the magazine with the postcard hidden inside. It might not matter to Simon if she fades into the ether, but it would matter to Deborah.

*

'We've all heard our illustrious lady Prime Minister expound on her vision of Britain – one of *truth* and *hope*.' The man is standing on a low platform at the far end of the room. He has no microphone, so has to shout to make himself heard at the back where Jenny stands. She can only see his head and shoulders above the crowd, but even at that distance, she can tell he is a small man trying to make himself look big.

'She has come to *save us*, she says. But she has not come to deliver us from the jaws of the sharks that feed on the workers of this nation. No! She's come, so she says, to save us from *ourselves*.' The man swaggers across the platform as he speaks, a Jack Russell pretending to be a Rottweiler. 'She makes no secret of her wish to destroy the trade union movement, and she won't hold back from destroying us with it. Just look what she's doing to the men of Port Talbot. She won't stop until every last one of them has been crushed. And then what? Who's next? I tell you now, there is no *truth* and there can be no *hope* as long as Margaret Thatcher is in Downing Street.' He comes to a stop in the centre of the stage, crosses his arms and stares at his audience.

'The workers' struggle has been a long one, my friends. And many of us are tired of fighting.' He speaks quietly now and the whole room strains to hear his words. Slowly, though, his voice grows stronger.

'We have been patient and loyal as we have waited for justice to come our way. Our dedication to our jobs and our families is what keeps this country going. None of us here want to see it fail. But our loyalty and hard work has made other men grow fat, while we are told to be grateful for the crumbs. Yes, it is the likes of us that keeps the country moving. But time is running out, and soon Thatcher will know that we can also bring it to a stop!' As he builds to a crescendo, the man raises both fists above his head and jabs the air with fingers pointed skyward. 'For five years, she has done her best to crush us. It's time for the workers of this country to rise up and take back control. I say: Where there is abuse of power, may we bring defiance. Where there is apathy, may we bring upheaval. Where there is oppression, may we bring resistance. And where there is tyranny, my friends, may we bring justice!'

Roger nudges Jenny as the crowd cheers its approval. He bends close to her ear. 'Listen to that, girl. We've got the power to bring this government down.' He shakes a fist in the air. '*Vive la révolution!*' He laughs. 'I almost wish I wasn't leaving.'

*

The ring flashes a tiny beam of light across the table, filling Jenny with a feeling of dread.

'That's nice,' she says, trying to sound casual. 'Is it from Ian?'

Charlotte retracts her fingers from her mug of tea and twists the ring, hiding the stone in the contours of her hand.

Jenny reaches out and pulls her daughter to her. It is the first time in months that Charlotte doesn't pull away from her touch and allows herself to be held. Jenny closes her eyes a moment and breathes in the scent of her daughter's hair. They should talk. Jenny should speak frankly, telling Charlotte about the many ways that men can disappoint; how the compliments and secret embraces eventually turn to silence and admonitions. She should say something about the way people change, about the speed at which the years pile up on one another, cementing life into unplanned designs. Charlotte needs to be prepared for what lies ahead. Doesn't she?

'You've obviously become very close over the summer.' She feels Charlotte's body grow tense, but does not loosen her hold. She must carry on, but slowly. She mustn't say too much too quickly and drive her only child away.

'Mum, you've known Ian nearly as long as I have.'

'Sure. But he's always just been one of your gang. Like Marilyn. Just a friend.'

'Yeah, well… now he's more than just a friend.'

Jenny takes a step back so she can see her daughter's face and combs her fingers through the wave of blonde hair that has fallen across her eyes. 'What does he think about you going to university? You'll be having all sorts of new experiences without him. You might come back with new expectations. You might even meet someone else.'

Charlotte pulls away abruptly, breaking Jenny's hold.

'And you'd like that, wouldn't you.'

*

Vera stands in the doorway, looking her up and down. 'You really should do something with your hair. Get it cut into a bob. Something more suitable for your age.'

Jenny didn't often go to her mother for advice – it seemed there were more things that divided them now than bound them together – and already she regrets stopping by the flat on her way home from work. She grits her teeth and smiles. 'Gee, Mum. It's good to see you, too.'

'I'm serious. You're getting to that age where you need to be careful. You're starting to look a bit... frumpy.'

It had been a spur-of-the-moment decision to come. For some reason she had thought her mother might be sympathetic, having raised a daughter of her own. She'd understand just how difficult it was at times. 'I came round for a chat, Mum, not abuse. If you're just going to criticise me I'll leave now.' Jenny glances towards the lift in the communal hall.

'Stay, stay,' Vera says. She waves Jenny into the flat, then follows her to the living room. 'Speaking my mind has always been my downfall. But not being able to take a bit of constructive criticism is yours. You want coffee? I'll put the kettle on.' She disappears into the adjoining kitchen without waiting for Jenny to answer.

The flat is small but tidy, just like her mother. There are no stray magazines on the sofa. No basket of laundry waiting to be folded and put away. Everything is dusted and polished and hoovered to perfection. Jenny looks around for somewhere to sit where she won't mess up the cushions, then crosses the room to stand at the window.

From the seventh floor, her mother's flat has a nearly unbroken view of the island, just visible above the rooftops of the guest houses and hotels on the seafront. Jenny traces the island's undulating backbone, and picks out the details of where she has been and where she still must go. As she ponders the distance between Ryde Pier and Osborne House, the sun catches the side of a cross channel ferry leaving the mouth of the harbour. She follows it as it glides past the war memorial and manoeuvres into the deeper water of the Solent. By suppertime, it will be in France.

'Come. Sit down.'

Jenny turns to see her mother carrying the coffee tray into the room. She seems thinner than Jenny remembers from just a week or two ago, and her back is slightly bent under the burden of the tray. She should make a point of visiting more often but their relationship has been prickly for years and the relief she feels when she leaves again is greater than the guilt. Still, her mother is getting older; she should make allowances. She should bite her tongue, and not feel goaded into responding to her mother's little jibes.

Vera sets the tray on the table in the corner and lays out two saucers and two cups and two side plates. She takes the lid off the tin of biscuits.

'Chocolate Hobnob?'

Jenny sits at the table facing her mother, takes two biscuits from the tin and sets them on her plate.

'Still not worried about your weight then, I see.'

Jenny feels the resentment welling up again, but pushes it down. 'Don't worry about me, I'm getting plenty of exercise these days.'

'Milk? Sugar?'

Jenny shakes her head. 'No, just black.'

Vera slides a cup of coffee across the table. 'There you go. No frills. No fuss. Just black.'

Somehow, even this feels like a criticism.

To her own cup, Vera adds a dash of milk, then takes up a little spoon and stirs until the coffee changes from black to nut brown. 'I always find a little milk makes it smoother.' She looks up at Jenny and smiles. 'Less bitter.'

Jenny would like to speak to her mother about Charlotte, about all the things she fears may happen and all the things she fears that won't. She would like to have someone to confide in. A woman. Someone who would understand. Someone who would empathise. It's the sort of relationship she wants with Charlotte. She takes a sip of her coffee. 'I was thinking about organising a meal for Charlotte's birthday. What's the name of that Italian place on London Road? The one with the waiters who sing and juggle plates.'

Vera rolls her eyes. 'Good Lord. You don't want to take her to that place, do you? She'd crawl under the table with embarrassment.'

'I thought it would be fun,' Jenny says. 'Something different.' She turns her eyes back to the window and gazes at the island in the distance. Why is everything so complicated?

Vera shakes her head. 'Trust me. She'd hate it. And she'll want to be with her friends, won't she? After all, she's got a lot to celebrate.'

Jenny wonders now if her mother knows about the ring. Has Charlotte phoned? Has she been round to show her? She takes a sip of her coffee, but leaves the biscuits untouched. 'Yes,' Jenny sighs. 'I suppose she has. Nineteen is a milestone. And then she'll be off to university.'

'Ah yes. University.' Vera raises an eyebrow. 'She's still going then, is she?'

Jenny feels annoyed by the question and fixes her eyes on her mother. 'Of course she is. That's always been the plan.'

There are little lines around her mother's lips – little wrinkles that stretch and almost disappear when she smiles, then deepen when she frowns. Vera shrugs. 'I would have thought she already knew enough English to get a job. Just how many verbs and adjectives does a person need these days?'

'That's not the only point of university, Mother. She can—'

Vera nods at the plate next to Jenny's coffee cup and cuts her off. 'Aren't you going to eat those now that you've taken them from the tin?' She reaches across the table and takes one of the biscuits from Jenny's plate, then snaps it in two and dips one of the halves in her coffee. The little wrinkles deepen as her lips reach out to receive it, then twist and split apart as she chews.

'Anyway,' Vera says, 'I've decided to buy her a little motor. Not a new one, of course. But a nice little runaround.'

'You're giving her a car? She can't even drive.'

Vera scoffs. 'Well, no, not yet. But she can learn. Simon is paying for her to take driving lessons for her birthday.'

'What?'

Vera smiles. 'He phoned the other day to tell me. Hasn't he said? He's going to help me choose the car. She'll need it, don't you think? Now she's engaged to be married.'

IV

It is Saturday again. A whole week has passed since Jenny first picked up the postcard and read the message on the back. A week since she set herself the task of finding Deborah. A week since she put everything at risk. And now she is making the crossing to the island again. To the east, the sky is flushed with the colour of marmalade and the sea, untroubled by even the slightest breeze, stretches glassy and silent and silver to the horizon. To the north, on the left-hand side of the ferry, a deserted funfair straddles Clarence Pier: the big wheel motionless, the cars of the rollercoaster parked and secure. Along the seafront, the common lies empty and behind it the dormant city stretches in a jagged outline of council blocks and sleeping seaside hotels. All is quiet now but for the screaming gulls that harry a fishing boat as it sails into the harbour. Across the water to the south, the island's silhouette spreads outwards in gentle waves.

As the ferry pushes its way through the thick water of the Solent, Jenny peers over the side. From above, the water is as black as a starless, midnight sky and she wonders about all of the men who have been pulled into its soundless depths: the bowmen and powder monkeys of the warship *Mary Rose*, yachtsmen and trawlermen; the despondent as well as the brave. She watches the ripples fan out around the boat, and feels herself drawn into the darkness, down into the underlying void of the sea, deeper and deeper until all she can see is nothing. There is comfort in giving up the struggle and her body is relaxed and weightless as the sea claims her and pulls her down.

The clang of a buoy bell breaks the silence and she quickly rises to the surface again. Looking up, she sees the island sliding towards her. With a bump, the ferry docks alongside Ryde Pier.

*

Jenny is the only passenger on the morning's first run as the train clatters its way south towards Shanklin. The carriage is old and worn, and the loose springs in the bench seats buck wildly as the train rattles and judders along the uneven track. Taken off-guard and nearly pitched into the aisle, Jenny allows herself to laugh out loud.

Outside, waves of amber corn roll past her window, and copses of narrow trees break the morning sunlight into diamonds. In the distance, an ancient oak, its twisted branches held wide against the horizon, stands like a sentinel at the centre of a wheat field: its forest brethren, axed long ago, turned to sailing ships or dovetailed beams, dining tables or smoke. The sight of it fills Jenny with an odd sadness. So much has been swept away; so much has been lost.

The train breathes out an airy whistle as rows of boxy houses spring up along the tracks on the approach to Brading. When it pulls into the station and comes to a stop, the doors slide open in unison, and for a moment the world is motionless and silent again. Jenny waits for someone to enter the carriage and break her seclusion. But no one boards the train and she resumes her journey alone.

*

Paolo was waiting at the entrance to the train station when she arrived, their tickets to Newhaven clasped in his hand. She was twenty minutes late when her bus pulled into the stop on the opposite side of the road, but she paused a moment to watch him – looking exotic and out of place in his flared trousers and long, camel hair coat. Even from a distance she could tell he was anxious by the way his eyes darted from one face to another, searching for her among the commuters, worried they would miss their train or that she might not come at all.

She had waited for her mother to leave for work that morning, tidying away the breakfast dishes as if it were any normal day, then locked the door behind her when she left the house and struggled beneath the weight of her rucksack to the bus stop on the corner. As the bus weaved its way through the city streets, its passengers shifting and changing at each stop, she imagined her mother searching the empty house when she returned home that evening, going from room to room until she found the letter on Jenny's bed, the letter that would tell her she was all alone. Jenny tried to shake the thought from her mind and imagine instead all of the adventures that lay ahead for her and Paolo. She tried to picture the two of them strolling arm in arm along leafy Parisian streets, looking as glamorous and worldly as Catherine Deneuve and Jean Marais. She tried to imagine them exploring ruined Greek temples, and swimming in the turquoise waters of *the Med*. They could go anywhere they wanted. The world was theirs. All they had to do was take the first step – and go!

But something wasn't quite right. The scenes in her head were hazy and imprecise, the images clipped from the travel pages of glossy magazines or borrowed from the films Paolo had taken her to London to see. No matter how hard she tried to picture the two of them together, her own face never quite fit. The only image that stood out in her mind was of her mother – all alone in an empty house.

Paolo hurried her through the station and on to the platform for their train, but the weight of the rucksack shifted awkwardly on her back, pitching her forward and from side to side until she thought she might stumble and fall. 'Wait!' she cried as they reached the train that would carry them to the ship that would sail them across the Channel to Dieppe. She pulled away from Paolo's pressing arm and came to a stop before she fell. They were nearly at their train. Another minute and they would be in the carriage, taking their seats. A few minutes later and the train would pull away from the platform and out of the station. A few minutes after that and they would be gone.

Jenny shook her head. 'I can't do this. I'm all she has.'

Paolo's voice was soft and reassuring. 'She's a grown woman, Jen. She'll be all right.'

She thought of the stiff new passport in a pocket in her bag, and how she had smelled the clean pages when it arrived in the post. She thought of the stamps it was meant to hold, a record of their adventures as they made their way around the world. They would have stories to tell their children, and stories to remember when they were old. That was the plan.

The sound of a whistle pierced the air. 'Would all passengers for the Brighton train please board now.' The conductor waited at an open door, just feet from where they stood. He checked his watch and nodded in their direction. 'The train is ready to depart.'

Paolo tugged at her arm, urging her forward. 'Come with me, Jen.' It was a plea, not a request or a command. 'Please, Jenny. Come with me.'

There was a whole world out there – across the water – just waiting to be explored. And Paolo was right. Her mother would survive just fine without her. She was perfectly capable of taking care of herself. Wasn't she?

'Come on, Jen! Let's go.'

Paolo tugged her arm once more, then reached for the carriage door and stepped aboard. He stretched an arm towards her. 'It's now or never.'

There were so many things she hadn't considered when they were mapping out their future. In the excitement of it all she'd failed to ask: *what if* and *what then* and *what about*? The conductor blew his whistle a final time and a door slammed closed. And when Jenny finally knew what it was she truly wanted, the train and Paolo were pulling away.

A moment later and they were gone.

Jenny opens her eyes and sees her bicycle on the other side of the aisle, propped against the empty seats of the Isle of Wight train. Out of the window she watches the outskirts of Sandown bleed into the last stop at Shanklin.

*

The phone box reeks of Friday-night piss. In the corner, beneath the phone itself, the paint has been bleached peppermint pink where it clings to the rust holding the panes of glass in place. One good shove is all it would take to dislodge the glass and let the air in but Jenny presses her foot against the door instead, holding it open a few inches as she pages quickly through the phone book. Still, the smell of ammonia burns in her throat. She runs her finger down the page of Cs until it stops at WB Cunningham. The address does not match, but she tries the number anyway. Somewhere down the line, a telephone rings, five, six, then seven times. Jenny holds her breath, waiting for a voice to interrupt the ringing. When no one answers, she puts the receiver down and leans into the door to breathe the fresh air again.

It is a quarter past eight in the morning and the town centre is empty apart from a flock of pigeons clustered round a discarded bag of last night's chips. When a seagull swoops down to join them, the pigeons rise from the pavement in a flurry of staccatoed wing-beats and scatter into the sky. Jenny finds a bench in the sun and sits a while, letting the stillness of the morning settle on her like a warm quilt on a cold day. For once, she has time to think. Tilting her head back to catch the sun, she inhales the cool sea air and holds it in her lungs until she feels herself beginning to float.

The sun is warm on her face and the thought of a youthful Simon flashes through her mind. Things were simple when the girls were small. Back then, all of life's injuries could be healed with a dab of

TCP and a kiss. And for a while, they had been the perfect family: two blossoming daughters, plans for the future, and money left over at the end of the week. They had everything they wanted then. They'd been happy. Satisfied. Certain that the future would be kind.

Then, overnight, they were hit by an unforeseen storm and the little vessel that had sustained them was capsized. Just when she needed it most, that *steady nature* her mother so admired about Simon was gone. He was powerless to keep them afloat. Since then, they'd been sinking a little further with each day that passed. How much longer did they have before they were completely submerged?

The sun is warm and comforting, and she is floating between two worlds, longing to move backwards in time when life was simple and complete. She feels his lips brush against the nape of her neck and opens her eyes. Suddenly, she is no longer hungry for his kiss.

The pink glow of sunrise is burnt away now and the sky is faintly blue, pale still, but growing bolder. Slowly, the town centre wakes up, rolls over and stretches: dog walkers and paperboys filter down the street; keys rattle as shop doors are unlocked and pushed open; tubes of fluorescent light flicker to life behind store windows. She looks around. There are people walking past who might know Deborah Cunningham. Or might know someone who does. All she has to do is find them.

*

If Deborah were her daughter, she would tell her to go to Michael and forgive him for whatever it was he said or did. Within reason, of course. That's what she'll say when she finds her. If you love him, and you're certain he loves you, that's all that matters. Grab on to this moment and don't let go. That's what she had wanted her own mother to say and it's what she wishes, really wishes, she could tell Charlotte. Chase after love while you can. Time passes so quickly. Don't waste it.

From her bench at the top of the high street, Jenny sees the red bicycle roll to a stop outside of the Co-op. She watches the postman set the kickstand, then peer into his post bag and gather a stack of letters into the crook of one arm. With his free hand he peels away the top few envelopes, ready for delivery, and enters the first of the row of shops. He's the person to ask about Edward Cottages, she thinks. He'll know his own route as well as he knows his own home and possibly a handful of other routes between Shanklin and Sandown besides. She'd have to be careful, though, not to say too much. And she daren't show him the card. He'd recognise it immediately for what it is – a dead letter – and start asking questions. No, she can't go to the postman for help. She waits until he leaves the shop and watches him enter the one next door, then begins to work her own way down the road.

The man behind the counter in the newsagent's pauses a moment to think out loud. 'Edward Cottages, eh? Let me see.' He strokes his chin and stares out of the window of his shop, clicking his tongue against the roof of his mouth. Finally, he puffs out his cheeks and turns back to Jenny. 'Nope. Sorry, love. Never heard of it. But why don't you ask old Clarence at the sweet shop?' He points along the street. 'He's lived here longer than most.'

When she leaves the shop, she spots the postman coming out of the butcher's a few doors along. He stops on the pavement and peels the next batch of envelopes from the stack in his arm. She can tell by his slow progress from one shop to the next that he enjoys a chat with the shopkeepers. He will know each of them by name, and most of their children as well. At the café at the bottom of the high street he probably stops for a cup of tea before crossing over the road and working his way back up the opposite row of shops, back to his bicycle parked at the top. If she asked him for help in finding the address, he would be glad to give her a few minutes of his time for he's in no particular hurry to finish his round. No hurry at all. Before he continues along his route, the postman glances back the way he has come and briefly meets Jenny's gaze. If she spoke to him now, she would soon have an answer to her question. Quickly, she looks away and darts through the door of the next shop.

By the time she has pushed her bicycle to the end of Regent Street, Jenny has queried eight people about Edward Cottages. In the sweet shop, Clarence had shaken his head and directed her to Elsie at the chemist's. 'I've only been here fifty years, but Elsie is Shanklin born and bred.' But Elsie had sent her to Betty in the dress shop, and Betty had sent her to Mary at the baker's. And Mary had directed her back to the newsagent's where she began. The day has barely started, but already Jenny feels exhausted by her search.

As the high street turns into Church Road Jenny weaves her way south out of Shanklin, swooping downhill before following the sign, left to Luccombe, and back to the sea. But the downhills never last long, and soon the road is climbing again. It winds in and out and around the shape of the land and seems far steeper going up than it was going down. She shifts down a gear. Then down again.

The morning is warm and growing warmer with the rising hill, but she presses on, ever hopeful that the next corner will reveal the top of the climb. Then, from behind her comes the metallic click of a racing bike changing gears, and a lean figure speeds past her right shoulder as if she were not moving forward at all. Ahead of her now, she sees the boy's blonde hair and black cycling shorts as he rises from the saddle. The bike tilts left and right with each quick pedal stroke, and countered by the movement of his shoulders the boy looks as if he is dancing on air. He is elegant and graceful. And so fast! Before he fades from view Jenny tries to follow his example, pulling herself into a standing position on the pedals and bearing down with all her weight. One stroke. Two. But she is moving slower, not faster, and her thighs are burning from the effort and she can barely breathe. The bike refuses to respond and gives in to the hill. She overbalances. She fails to catch herself. She topples into the verge. Lying in the grass at the side of the road, she feels old and cumbersome, another species from the sleek-bodied boy.

Catching her breath, she pushes herself up and back on to her feet, and it is then that she notices the view. She pauses a moment to take it in, tracing the line of the coast as it curves behind her, rising up into chalk cliffs and thrusting into the tide. The water that stretches into the distance now is cobalt blue, almost black. Against the darkness of the empty sea the sails of a lone sailboat flash like a beacon. She lifts her bike from the ground, turns to the road again, and begins to push.

*

The racing bike is leant against a wooden stile beside the road, but the graceful boy is nowhere in sight when she reaches the top of the hill. Back along the coast, only a faint line of the mainland is visible beyond the cliffs at Culver Down. Jenny searches the increasing expanse of water until she finds the sailboat, smaller now and further away, heading out to sea.

Along the green line of the footpath that cuts across the field and leads to the edge of the cliff, the young cyclist strides towards her. He is angular and loose-limbed with bony elbows and knees, and off the bike his gait is awkward and self-conscious, as though he is not quite sure of his legs.

'If you're hoping to find a better view down there, I shouldn't bother.' He glances behind him as he approaches the stile. 'Too much gorse and bramble blocking the edge. The best view is right here.'

She sees now that he is Charlotte's age, young enough to be her son. Still growing into the man he will become.

'It's a tough ride, isn't it?' He nods towards the hill they have both climbed. 'Especially with hub gears.' He looks at the bike she has leant next to his. 'Did you really ride all the way to the top? That's pretty impressive if you did.'

Jenny shakes her head. 'No. I guess I'm not much of a cyclist.'

'You're on a bike, aren't you? That's all that counts.' He grins and looks out across the view again. 'The pain is worth it when you get to the top, though. Don't you think?'

Jenny follows his line of sight. She searches for the sailboat, again, but cannot find it on the dark sea. 'Yes, I suppose it is.'

'Whenever I get to the top of this climb I think I'm *king of the mountain*. I can do anything.' He laughs and flexes his thin arms. 'Know what I mean?' He glances once more at the sea, then grabs his bike and spins it round so that it faces the road again, back the way he has come.

Jenny shakes her head. The boy has ridden all the way up this hill only to go back down it again.

'Are there more hills this steep?' She hears the desperation in her own voice and bites her lower lip, embarrassed. 'I wish I had your confidence.'

He laughs again. 'You're not from around here, are you? Don't worry. I'll tell you a secret. If your head believes you can get to the top, your body will follow.' He taps his forehead with a finger. 'The hills are tough, but you know something? I think you're tougher. After all, you're up here, aren't you? If you made it this far, you can make it the rest of the way.'

Then, in one smooth motion, he presses down on a pedal and throws his free leg over the back of the bike, and before Jenny has time to ask how she can make herself believe the impossible he is gliding away from her. A moment later, and he is gone.

The road moves steeply up again and she is back to pushing her bike, betrayed by another false summit and the young man's smile. Rounding another corner, the tarmac ends abruptly and empties on to a dry mud road. A sign announces that she has reached 'The Highway'. Glancing over her shoulder, the view has changed once more. Hills flow out of one another, darkly green against the now silver sea. Ahead of her, the track narrows into a footpath and cuts upwards through a field of hillside sheep. 'Bloody hell,' she says, reaching for her map.

She finds Shanklin again and traces her finger along the road which had led her out of town. It was the downhill that had enticed her into turning left, and now she sees that the route she took was always going to come to an end. She should have kept to the main road, braving the traffic and the long, gradual climb. Now, the only options she has are going back the way she has come and returning to the A3055 or following the footpath up the grassy hillside to the unseen road at the top. Turning back would mean she'd climbed the hill for nothing. Gritting her teeth, she hefts her bike on to her shoulder and clambers over the stile into the field and starts making her slow way up the footpath towards the road at the top of the hill.

By the time she reaches the road again, Culver Down and Culver Cliffs lie half-hidden behind a screen of broadleaf trees, and the mainland has vanished entirely. But beyond the trees and the fields and the hills, the sea stretches out forever. She searches briefly for the little white sailboat, but it is far too small now, and the sea is far too vast.

Back on her bicycle, she sees the road drop away like an unwound ribbon, folding back on itself and hugging the shape of the hills. Jenny back-pedals a quarter turn so that her feet rest parallel to the ground and she crouches low to the handlebars as the boy on the racing bike had done, and chases the ribbon downhill.

As she picks up speed, the fast-flowing air against her skin and the anticipation of falling too fast thrills her more than she had expected. The struggle to the top of the hill is forgotten now. She holds tightly on to the handlebars but all her fear is gone, and she does not reach for the brakes. Her body is weightless as she soars down the hill and remembers the last time she was able to fly.

The room in her mind is pink with fairy lights and chiffon, and she is seven years old again, spinning round and round, delighted by the way her party dress lifts and billows out around her legs. She spins so fast that she becomes a flower, plucked and thrown on the wind, turning and twirling and floating in the air, giddy with the freedom of flight. Her father's voice rings in her ears, laughing with her as she dances. He claps his hands to the rhythm of her heartbeat – so fast, so fast! And when she grows dizzy and her wings are too weak to carry her through the air, he reaches out and catches her just as she begins to fall.

*

The road drops down and further down, further than she wants to go, down into Bonchurch and down towards the sea once more. Now as she falls, the thrill of flying has left her. She reaches for the brakes to slow her descent, but the road is still falling away. Every inch of the hill she gained she is now about to lose, and she curses the downhill more than she ever cursed the climb. The road will soon rise up again and her struggles will resume. She slows past the Ramblers, Rose Cottage, and the Beeches, checking for a glimpse of Edward Cottages at every corner and driveway. She must not forget why she's here.

The stone walls of Bonchurch village shade the main road from the hot summer sun. Now, though, they seem to shroud the day with an early dusk. Above the slate-grey rooftops and above the walls, the hills beyond the village loom like battlements. Jenny eyes them warily. Their presence darkens her thoughts as they do the high street.

She had been ten years old when her father left. He'd kissed the top of her head that morning, just as he always did as he left the house to go to work, but at the end of the day when they should have been sitting down together for supper he still hadn't returned home. Within a week, every remnant of him, every photograph which held his face, every piece of clothing he wore, everything that bore his image or his scent, everything that bore his handwriting, even, had been stripped from the house. The only thing left to keep his face alive in Jenny's memory was the photograph she'd hidden when the others began to disappear. Her mother had erased him from their lives as ruthlessly as a cup of bleach in a bucket of water removes tea stains from taffeta. And then, like the taffeta, their lives fell apart.

The road snakes past the foot of St Boniface Down and winds its way into Ventnor before curling up on itself at a point where it can drop no further. With her back to the hill, Jenny sits on a bench on the Esplanade and gazes out to sea. The water is opaque now with the reflection of the heat-hazed white sky and it draws her into its emptiness, into a space where time can be submerged and forgotten, ignored or remembered.

The things she and Simon shared had dwindled away over the past two years, and now all they talk about are the trivialities of life: the Sunday roast; *that bloody dog next door*; the weather. Anything deeper than a paper cut leads to conflict. And they can't deal with conflict any more. Their nerve-endings lie too close to the surface for that.

Soon, Charlotte will be gone and it will just be the two of them at home. The thought of the empty rooms and all that silence presses down on her. In a month, she'll be forty. *Forty years old.* She's young enough to start again, she thinks. Isn't she? Or has she had her life now? *Is this it?* Charlotte no longer needs her – her usefulness as a mother is spent. And Simon? He, too, would manage without her. Who knows – he might even flourish.

She pushes the thoughts away and looks around for a phone box. She isn't totally redundant yet. She still has one job she needs to do. Deborah is waiting. She just needs to find her.

The route out of Ventnor angles sharply uphill. A sign at the bottom gives it an apt name: Zig Zag Road. Jenny eyes the tarmac as it rises up the hill, turning back on itself in a series of tight corners. There is no point even getting on the bike this time. Placing one foot in front of the other, she slowly pushes herself and the bicycle forward.

Half an hour later, she reaches the top, her legs and back aching from the climb. Pausing to stretch and catch her breath, she checks her map to get her bearings and looks around. There's so much to take in: the sea, the sky, the road, the hills. Far below her now, the sea spreads out in every direction, changing from turquoise to silver to cobalt blue. From where she stands it is all just so... *immense*. As she scans the shimmering water, her eyes are drawn to the horizon where the sea bends and flows away to unseen foreign shores and she wonders if she will ever know what really lies out there, beyond that narrow line that divides sea from sky.

Facing the road again, she ponders her route. The A3055 lies behind her now, hugging the coast as it travels on to St Lawrence and the west side of the island. She will go that way another time, but for now she must turn inland, looping her way back in the direction of Ryde.

The road passes a string of blonde- and red-brick houses as she rides north away from town, then glides along the top of the downs, dipping and cresting on the swells of the barley-stubbled hills. The road is smooth, with bramble and hawthorn lining either side. In places, the hedges are so overgrown and the beech trees and blackthorn are so thick they entwine overhead to form a tunnel, and for a few moments at a time she is caught within the broken, flickering, magical light that shines through their leaves. Now and then, a gateway or a gap appears in the hedge, allowing glimpses of sheep or grazing black-and-white cows. The day is warm and the scent of moist grass and freshly turned soil fills the air. In the distance a hawk hangs in the sky, its wings barely moving.

She rolls through Wroxall and Whiteley Bank, past village shops and twee flint cottages and farmhouses and country pubs, and is a mile past Apse Heath before she realises she has not stopped to ask after Deborah, did not even think of her or glance at the names of the houses she has passed. The road has mesmerised her. For a moment, she considers turning round. But the call to keep going, to feel the movement of the earth beneath her, is stronger than the call to go back and she presses on to Sandown. There, on the busy seafront, she sees again the smooth green back of Culver Down and the point where the land spills into the sea.

Brading is smaller than it looks on the map, but Deborah could be here all the same, just up the street or round the corner. On the pavement outside the village hall, Jenny scans the cards on the community noticeboard, looking for something that might help in her search. *Guitar Lessons, £5 an hour; Will do ironing; Room to rent – ladies only.* Nothing. In her hand she holds Michael's postcard. She has read it more than a dozen times in the past week, but she reads it again, searching for clues. His words are written in small, angular letters that are unhurried and precise. He has taken care over the message to make sure its meaning is clear. At the bottom of the card, he has printed his name in block capitals rather than signing it with his usual flourish. His words are contrite, and he wants nothing to distract Deborah from his regret. He's doing everything in his power to make her understand. He was wrong. He's sorry. And he's desperate not to lose her. *Life is nothing without you in it.*

'If you ask in the village shop, they'll be happy to pin that up for you.'

Jenny looks up to find a woman not much older than herself peering over her shoulder.

'Oh, sorry,' the woman says, looking closer at the postcard. 'I thought you had something you wanted to sell.' She smiles and gestures across the road. 'There's a postbox if you need one.'

Jenny shakes her head and the woman begins to move away, but she speaks quickly to stop her from leaving. 'No – but perhaps you can help me with something.'

Turning back, the woman glances at the card again. She has kind eyes, Jenny thinks. She can trust her. She'll understand.

Without thinking, Jenny thrusts the card towards her, but before the woman reaches out to receive it, she wishes she could grab it back. She is being impulsive and reckless again. For all she knows, this woman – this *stranger* – whom she has just met on the street might work for Royal Mail. Or the police. She might recognise the crime that's been committed. She's certain to ask questions. *And then... and then...* The woman takes the card and looks briefly at the beach. Jenny's heart is racing, but when the woman turns the card over and glances up as if for approval, Jenny nods. 'Go ahead. You can read it.'

Jenny watches the woman's eyes skim the message, then pause and start again, moving across the words more slowly this time. When she is finished, the woman lays a hand against her heart. 'Young love can be so painful. But I'm not sure I understand.'

'The address,' Jenny says. 'Do you recognise it?'

The woman looks again, then nods. 'Ah yes.' She purses her lips and seems to consider the problem for a moment. Finally, she shakes her head and hands the postcard back. 'But where did you find it?' Jenny feels suddenly sick, but before she can think of an answer, the woman comes up with her own. 'The postman must have dropped it. Is that it? Some of them just don't care. I'm forever getting my neighbour's letters posted through my door.'

Jenny releases the breath she has been holding and returns the card to the safety of the *Woman's Own*. 'I thought I might be able to find the address if I asked around. Seemed a shame not to try. But I'm not having much luck.'

The woman frowns. 'Sounds like you're on a wild goose chase if you ask me.'

Jenny sighs. 'Yes, it seems that way.'

'But that's not necessarily a bad thing, is it? I've always liked an adventure myself.'

On her way down the high street, Jenny stops another half a dozen times to ply people with questions, making sure the card remains firmly in its place. When she leaves the village she feels no closer to her objective, but somehow it doesn't matter. The sky is blue and the sun is warm on her back, and each bend in the road reveals a new surprise. She is indeed on an adventure. And it's not a bad thing at all.

Weaving her way on to Bembridge, the sea, St Helens and Nettlestone, she is finally back at Ryde Pier, back to where the day began.

Evening is approaching but still there are holiday-makers parading along the Esplanade, and dings and whistles and ringing bells spill from the arcade across the street. A little boy wearing red jelly shoes skips past the bench where she sits while she waits for the ferry to arrive. He clutches a plastic windmill in his hand and it spins on the breeze as he runs.

Simon will be wondering where she is by now. Surely he will. Perhaps he'll have phoned her mother. Perhaps they'll both be worried. As she waits for the ferry, she unfolds her map and traces her route so far. She has covered half of the coast on the north side of the island, and most of that on the east. When she returns tomorrow, she'll make another loop, from Ryde out to Freshwater on the western tip, then back through Newport to see Lily again. And if she doesn't find Deborah tomorrow, she still has the long bank holiday weekend at the end of the month.

V

Rain is lashing against the window when Jenny wakes on Sunday morning and when she draws back the curtains in the living room the world outside looks as if it has melted around the edges. The steeliness of the clouds tells her it's not just a passing shower. The rain will continue for some time yet, and when it does eventually subside and the sky pales to the colour of ash, it will be replaced by a drizzle that could last for days. She lets the curtain fall back into place. She still has next weekend to find Deborah, and the bank holiday Monday as well. Three days. That's still enough time.

She hopes.

*

'Have you heard the whispers?' Roger sets a full box of letters on his bench and leans in close.

Jenny shakes her head and glances over her shoulder as she continues to work. 'What's going on?'

His voice is low, barely audible above the noise of the machines. 'Mick Jones has been given the sack.'

'Oi! You're not being paid to chit-chat down there!' Taylor's voice bellows down the aisle.

Roger upends the box of letters and begins sorting at a casual pace.

'Tricky Mick has been sacked?' Jenny looks around to see an unfamiliar figure standing at Mickey's usual frame.

'They said he was slipping coins out of birthday cards. Caught him with a pocket full of change. That was their only evidence.'

She continues flicking letters into her frame. 'He's been stealing birthday money from kids?'

'Course not. You know Mickey. He wouldn't do a thing like that. I know he's a bit of a wide boy, but he wouldn't stoop that low.'

She glances at the blackened windows overhead. 'They must have had some kind of proof, don't you think? Someone must have seen something.'

Roger nods his head in Taylor's direction. 'My guess is, Mick's sold a dodgy radio to someone down there and they've stitched him up. The union's calling for a strike unless he's reinstated. There's a meeting tomorrow for a show of hands. We could be out on the street by Friday.'

Jenny pauses a moment and looks at Roger. 'Can that happen? So quickly, I mean?'

'If they think it's unfair dismissal the union boys can whip things up pretty fast. We're not just talking about Mickey, here. None of our jobs are safe. Just look at what's happening in Wales. The government's putting pressure on unions all over the place. The country's getting ready to explode.'

'Come on, Roger. Wales is different. The miners have a reason to strike. Mick Jones wouldn't stick his neck out to help me. Why do I care if he gets the sack?' A week after taking the card, she has only just started to relax. Now her stomach is in knots.

'We were out for eight weeks during the big strike of '71.' Roger chuckles to himself and idly continues pitching envelopes into pigeonholes. 'Brought the country to a stop, we did.'

Jenny's thoughts turn to the postcard tucked away safely in her bedside drawer. If someone had seen her take it, she'd have been sacked by now, like Tricky Mickey. Still, she needs to be careful.

'So what do you think?'

She holds a letter in mid-air and shrugs her shoulders. 'You know what things are like at home.'

'Look, Jen.' Roger's voice has taken on a serious tone. 'If we let them get away with sacking Mick, any one of us might be next. All they'll need is a hint of suspicion. Not proof. Do you hear what I'm saying? If they even suspect something isn't kosher they'll hit first and ask questions later.'

*

The pub is tucked away on a side street a few minutes' walk from the sorting office, and once or twice a week they sit at a corner table and wait for the world to settle into place. A dozen regulars are scattered around the room: flat-capped pensioners sitting at separate tables on their own, and dockyard workers on the dole nursing pints of brown beer at the bar. Above them, a ghostly tide of cigarette and pipe smoke churns in the air. Jenny lifts the half-pint of bitter shandy Roger has set on the beer mat in front of her and takes a long drink.

'So now, me girlie, tell your Uncle Roger what it is that's bothering you.'

Jenny closes her eyes and leans back against the wooden bench seat, rolling the glass back and forth between the palms of her hands as she collects her thoughts.

'You haven't been yourself, lately, Jen. Something's happened to stir you up. Just look at yourself.'

She opens her eyes. 'Is it that obvious?'

Roger nods. His lips form a straight, thin line across his face as he leans across the table. 'Listen,' he whispers, 'if it's about the postcard, I don't think anyone else saw you take it.'

She stares at him a moment then turns her head away and studies the men at the bar. They lean heavily on their elbows, in ones and twos, their broad backs forming a wall around the woman pulling pints.

'It's not like you to do something like that, Jen. If Taylor had seen you, he'd have had your backside out the door before you could turn round. And he'd have been right to do it.'

She turns back towards Roger, but she can't meet his eyes. 'I know. I know. It was stupid. You don't have to tell me.'

'So why'd you do it?'

She runs a finger across the puckered impression of a cigarette burn on the table. 'It had an incomplete address.'

'Right. And?'

'It seemed urgent. I thought I could help. I thought I could deliver it faster than the guys in Dead Letters.'

Roger leans back in his chair. 'I hope you know what you're doing, kid. Fixing other people's problems sounds like a full-time job to me.'

She finishes her shandy and stares into the empty glass.

'Looks like this is going to be a long session.' Roger pushes his chair back from the table and stands. 'You sit there and decide what you want to say and I'll get another round in.'

'Leave out the lemonade this time, will you.'

Jenny watches Roger cross the room. He nods at a couple of posties walking through the door and together they join the bank of men standing at the bar. In the early days, when she first went to work in the sorting office, it was Roger who had shown her the ropes: how to stand for an hour without her knees locking up; how to fend off the innuendoes and the sniping of the other men. He never grew impatient with her questions. And she can't remember all the times he's stood up for her when Taylor's tried to push her around. In the five years they've worked together, he's become a good friend. And now she can't bear the thought of him leaving for Australia and never coming back.

When he returns with the drinks the words are still jumbled in her head. How does she begin teasing them apart and placing them in an order that someone else can understand? It's not the postcard that fills her mind. *That* is just a distraction. It's not even Simon – though he, too, is tangled up in that knot somewhere, so that is where she will start. She waits for Roger to settle again, then takes a deep breath and begins.

'He's a good man,' she says. 'I don't deserve him.'

Roger strokes his stubbled chin, thoughtfully. 'I always suspected you had a soft spot for Taylor.'

Jenny looks up from her glass and smiles.

'You know, kid,' he says softly, 'that sounds like something a person might say when they're getting ready to walk out on hard times.'

Jenny looks past his shoulder at the men at the bar, and takes a sip of her beer. 'Yeah,' she whispers, 'maybe it does.'

'Listen, love.' Roger reaches across the table and squeezes her fingers. 'I don't even want to imagine what you and Simon have been through the last couple of years. What you're still going through.

But you just have to stick with it. It takes time. It's nearly six years now that Frankie's been gone and there isn't a day go by that I don't still miss her. It's still hard, but it's not as bad as it was. Give it time.'

Roger is only trying to help – she knows this – repeating the words people use when they don't know what else to say. She's heard them all before, a hundred times. But so far, nothing has got any easier.

She forces a smile to her lips. 'I'm okay,' she says. 'We both are. We're managing, anyway.'

'And Charlotte? How's she, these days?'

'Charlotte?' Jenny rolls her eyes. 'Charlotte is *in love*.' In her head, the words have a lightness and buoyancy, but as they emerge into the open they quickly deflate. 'She's engaged now. Apparently.'

Roger laughs. 'It was bound to happen sooner or later. Scary, though, isn't it?'

She takes a drink of her beer. 'They grow up so qui—' She catches herself mid-sentence. 'Well. She'll be nineteen next week. She's an adult now.'

Silence settles over them as their thoughts drift off in different directions for a time, and little by little, the words that have been so tightly tangled in Jenny's head begin to loosen.

'Everything changed after we lost Sophie.' She hesitates and looks up. She finds it hard to speak about her youngest daughter now, though Sophie is never far from her mind. But her *death*... somehow it's at the root of everything that has followed, and so she must continue by returning to the source.

'Simon seemed to shut down after Sophie died. There were times when I just needed him to hold me and tell me everything was going to be okay... that's all I needed – that's all I wanted him to do. But he didn't. And I couldn't ask.' She pauses, trying now to remember the things she has tried to forget. 'He was so fragile. I didn't know how to help him. And he didn't know how to help me. So we didn't talk about it – about what happened – even though it infected every part of our lives. It surrounded us. It got inside of us. And after a while, I guess we just got used to being broken.' She gazes at an old man at a table nearby. He seems so calm, so content with his newspaper and his pint of beer. 'We couldn't help each other. And we couldn't help Charlotte, either.'

She presses her fingers against the burn mark again. But no matter how much she rubs it, it won't go away. 'I've failed her, Roger. Just like I failed her sister.'

*

'I've changed my mind. About university.'

They are standing in the kitchen with their backs to one another: Jenny filling the kettle at the sink, Charlotte rummaging through the refrigerator for breakfast.

'Sorry, love, I missed that.' Jenny switches the kettle on and turns to look at her daughter.

Charlotte straightens to inspect a pot of yoghurt. 'Ugh. Rhubarb.' She yawns and stretches, then shoves the yoghurt to the back of the fridge again. 'I don't know how you manage these early shifts. The sun isn't even up yet.'

Jenny places two mugs on the counter. 'You get used to it. And you'll be glad for the extra money, once you're off to uni.'

Charlotte sets a pint bottle of milk on the counter, closes the fridge door and scrutinises the shelves in the cupboard. She picks up the box of cornflakes and gives it a shake. 'I'll pick up some groceries after work, shall I? We seem to be running low on the essentials.' She sets the box on the table and returns to the cupboard. 'And Mum – I've just told you. I've changed my mind. I'm not going to university.'

Jenny stares blankly at her daughter's back. 'You mean you're deferring? A lot of people take a year out these days. To work or travel.'

Charlotte sets a cereal bowl by the cornflakes, at one end of the table. 'No, Mum. I mean I'm not going. Just that. I didn't get the results I needed for Southampton. Okay?'

'You've had your results? Already?'

Charlotte snatches one of the mugs Jenny has selected and returns it to the shelf above the kettle, replacing it with another bearing her name: *Charlotte!* 'Yes, Mum. They came out last Thursday. You really haven't been paying attention lately, have you? It was on the calendar. See?' Without looking round, Charlotte points at the calendar next to the kitchen door.

Jenny follows the line of her daughter's out-stretched arm to find a single date, 16 August, ringed in red. The word *RESULTS* is printed boldly in the box. As the kettle rumbles and clicks off, Charlotte glides round her, dropping teabags into the mugs and collecting spoons from the cutlery drawer.

'But... but why didn't you say anything on the day? Why didn't you remind me?'

The spoons clatter noisily on to the table. 'It's okay, Mum. Don't worry about it. It's not a big deal. You've been busy.'

Jenny's body is rigid, but her head is reeling. *How could she have forgotten?* 'Well, go on. Tell me. What did you get? Your results can't have been that bad. Surely you can get a place somewhere else. Through Clearing. Isn't that what they call it? Southampton isn't the only university... We'll make some phone calls and find out what we need to do.'

Charlotte switches the kettle on again, waits for it to boil, and pours water into both of the mugs. 'Listen, Mum, I've changed my mind. Okay? Maybe I could go somewhere else, but I don't want to move halfway across the country and spend the next three years studying something that won't even get me a job. What could I do with an English degree, anyway? Ian and I are getting a flat. We're planning to tell Dad tonight.'

Jenny winces as something within her suddenly contracts. 'Oh, sweetheart. You're still so young, and it's such a big thing – getting engaged. Living with someone. I thought we decided it would be better to wait until you finished your education.'

Charlotte adds a spoon of sugar to each of the mugs, pushes the teabag in her own back and forth a few times, then spoons it out and drops it in the sink, repeating the process for Jenny's. 'No, Mum, *you* decided it would be a good thing to wait. And now I have. Okay?' She pours milk into the mugs, then leans against the counter, facing her mother for the first time.

Jenny tries to measure her words before she speaks them. As Charlotte has grown up and become bolder, she herself has grown more cautious, aware of all that lies at risk between her and her eldest and now only daughter. 'Your father and I, we've been so… so proud of you, love. The last couple of years have been hard on all of us. But you did so well at college, despite everything. Shouldn't we at least sit down with your dad and talk about this before you decide?'

'I'm almost *nineteen*, Mother. I don't need you to tell me what I should do with my life. I'm tired of you always trying to control things. Ian and I have decided to move in together, and that's that. Dad will understand. You'll see. *He* likes Ian.'

Though Jenny loves her daughter, she is concerned that she might not like her. She's become distant and scornful. And nothing Jenny does is ever good enough any more. But now, one thought dominates all others: if she no longer has Sophie, and if Simon and now

Charlotte are both slipping away, she'll soon be left with nothing. Everyone she's ever loved will be gone. She has to think quickly, before it's too late.

'But a degree will give you options. It will get you a better job. You could go places and do things most people could only dream of. Remember all the plans you made about going to Australia? You were going to get to know your cousins. You were going to travel and see the world. You shouldn't throw all that away without a thought.'

Charlotte sighs, loudly. 'You haven't been listening, have you? Australia was your idea, not mine. Besides, I *have* thought about it. And I've made up my mind. It's not your decision to make.'

Jenny feels herself grasping for something to keep her afloat. 'But you're such a clever girl, Charlotte. And you've worked so hard.'

Charlotte stands up straight and looks her in the eye. Long-legged and slim, she has taken after Simon in more ways than one. Her eyes are cold, and it's all Jenny can do to keep herself from turning away.

'You're right,' Charlotte says, her voice suddenly unleashed. 'I have worked hard. And you know what I've learned? No matter how hard I study, my grades still won't be good enough. Things were easy for Sophie. She was the clever one, not me. If I went to university, I'd always be struggling to keep up.'

'But Charlotte…'

'No, Mother. This is my life.' She hesitates as though she's sorting through all the unspoken words, selecting the most destructive. 'Sophie was the one who was going to live out all your dreams.' Her voice shakes as the words spill out. 'But I'm not like Sophie.' Her breath has become shallow and rapid. She crosses her arms across her chest and hugs herself tightly. 'What you're really saying is that I'm not good enough for you. Well you know what? That's not my problem. It's your life that's a mess, not mine. It's no wonder Dad is so miserable. Just look at yourself. You need to sort out your own life and leave me to get on with mine.'

Charlotte's aim is perfect. She knows just where the soft spots are, and she flings her words with devastating force.

'Stop trying to turn me into Sophie.' She glares at her mother. 'Sophie is dead!'

Jenny recoils from the impact. 'No!' Instinctively, she raises her hand to fend off the attack, and slaps her daughter hard across the face.

Jenny's fingers sting, and she stares at her hand as if she has not seen it before. 'Oh God,' she says. 'Charlotte, I'm sorry.'

All she has ever wanted was to protect her children, to guide them in the right direction. To keep them from harm. But now, all of her fears are coming true. She has lost one daughter and is driving the other away.

Charlotte doesn't cry out. Nor does she touch the red bloom spreading across her cheek. Her eyes are fixed on her mother's, and when Jenny reaches out to her she shakes her hands loose and pulls away.

'Get off me,' she hisses.

Jenny covers her face with her hands. 'I'm sorry,' she whispers.

And when she looks up again, Charlotte is gone.

*

Tipton, Purbrook, Tavistock, Ross; Sherbourne, Botley, Bosham, Bath. She feels sick, knows the cause of it, but cannot undo what has already been done. At the end of the line, a radio is playing, but Jenny is too far away to hear it. Now and then, a note forces its way through the rumble of the CFC, like an air bubble rising from the sea bed, bursting into life for one brief moment then instantly dying back. She strains to capture enough of the tune that she can carry on humming to herself, but the noise of the machinery drowns everything but her own thoughts.

*

It's almost dusk when she arrives home from work, but no lights shine through the windows of the house and she wonders if anyone else is in as she turns her key. She'd stayed late at work again, doing an extra half shift on top of her own to delay coming back to this sort of silence.

But the house is not perfectly still after all, and as she pushes the front door closed behind her, she hears the muffled voices in the living room. She pauses in the hall a moment and listens. The television, of course. Simon is on the sofa, asleep in the dusk now, but maintaining a pose of alertness. Jenny studies him from the doorway. She can see, even in this half-light, that his face is puffy and red. He's been crying.

He stirs as she enters the room, and calls out, 'Charlotte, is that you?'

'No, Simon, it's me.' Then reading the panic in his voice, she draws a sharp intake of air. 'What's happened? Where is she?'

He reaches out, and without hesitation she goes to him. 'She's not been home all day.' His voice begins to quake and he draws in a deep breath. 'She was already gone when I woke up, and she didn't come back from work. She didn't leave a note. She hasn't phoned. It's not like her, Jen. Something's happened, I'm sure.'

Jenny's mind races back to the morning. They had both been getting ready for work. Charlotte was doing her first early shift at Tesco. Working six until two.

She slips down to sit beside him and holds him in her arms. She needs to remain calm. But Simon is right. It isn't like her. Charlotte knows how much they worry about her now. She always, *always* phones if she's going to be late. Jenny peers over Simon's shoulder and checks the clock on the wall. She should have been home hours ago. Taking a deep breath, she pushes her fears to the back of her mind. She has to stay calm.

She presses Simon's face to her shoulder and feels his breath upon her neck. She finds in its warmth a type of comfort that settles her and helps her to think. It feels good to hold him like this. It feels good to be needed.

'No,' she says, piecing her thoughts together. 'I'm sure she's fine. I'm sure everything is all right.' She thinks again about the morning. She thinks again about the slap. 'Charlotte's angry. With me. That's all it is. We had a row. I'm sure she's just trying to avoid me for a while.'

Jenny takes a deep breath and releases it slowly, and when she speaks again her voice is hesitant and thin. 'We were both angry.' She can tell he's listening by the stillness of his body. She can barely feel his breath against her skin. 'She said something that upset me and… I lost it for a minute.' She closes her eyes and remembers the sting in her fingers. 'I slapped her,' she whispers.

Simon pulls away and looks at her. 'You did what?'

His eyes are full of sorrow and doubt and she wonders how long they've been this way. 'I… I shouldn't have done it,' she says quickly. She remembers the stab of Charlotte's words – *Sophie's dead!* – but can't bring herself to repeat them. 'She says she's not going to university. She wants to live with Ian.'

Simon nods. 'Yes, she does. And that's why you slapped her?' His eyes seem to be searching her for something more.

Jenny lowers her head. 'I'm afraid she's rushing things. Aren't you?'

He sighs loudly but seems to relax again, letting his body sink back into place against hers. 'It's hard, isn't it?' he whispers. 'Watching her grow up. Knowing what to say and what not to say. Doing the right thing.' He slips an arm around her and draws her close. 'She's disappointed with her results more than she's letting on. We'll talk to her, tomorrow.'

Simon's right. Charlotte is a sensible girl. And Jenny needs to learn to trust her. 'If she lived at home, she could save up and go to uni next year. But all she can think about is Ian. And now... and now they're engaged to be married?'

'Ian's not such a bad bloke, you know. She could do far worse.'

'He's got you smoking again. I've smelled it on your breath.'

He strokes the back of her head as she nuzzles into him. 'I've only had a couple, Jen. Just to be sociable.'

His heartbeat is steady and reassuring, and she wishes they could stay locked together like this forever. 'I'm just afraid she'll miss out. That she'll regret settling down too soon. That Ian won't stick around. Or worse – that he will.'

*

Nestled together within the soft folds of the duvet, they had been roused from their sleep by the sound of Charlotte's footsteps on the stairs. Simon had pulled Jenny close. 'We'll talk to her in the morning,' he whispered, and she had finally let go and found sleep. Now, as daylight finds its way through the bedroom curtains, she rests her head in the crook of his arm and lets herself doze a while longer, not wanting the spell to be broken. *Maybe, just maybe they can still make this work.*

*

'I didn't see you at the meeting last night.'

Roger's voice cuts into her thoughts as she launches a letter towards the frame. She watches the envelope hit the edge of the pigeonhole and fall to the bench, and glances at him with a teasing, accusatory look. 'Watch it! You're putting me off my stride.'

Now that Roger is there, her rhythm slows to an easy pace that matches his. 'Yeah, sorry,' she says as letters flow into the frame. 'I forgot.'

'Mickey claims he was set up by one of the managers. We voted for a walkout. This morning at ten.'

Jenny looks at Roger as she reaches for the Manchester box in the top right corner of her frame. 'I'm going on strike because of Mickey Jones?' She holds the letter in mid-air for a moment, then drops her hand and taps the envelope on her bench.

'Come on, Mickey's not as bad as some folks like to make out. Besides, you should have been at the meeting if you wanted to vote against it. It was a democratic decision.'

Jenny flings the Manchester letter into its pigeonhole, then casts another towards Salisbury.

'I guess it slipped my mind. There's been a lot going on at home.'

Roger nods as letters flow from his hand.

'Anyway,' he says, 'I thought you were all for the union.'

'I *am*,' she says. 'But are you sure Mickey isn't just an excuse? The union has been itching to take us on strike for months.'

She finishes sorting the letters in her hand, then scoops up those that have fallen to the bench and places them in their pigeonholes one by one. 'So we're walking out then.'

'Yep,' Roger says, checking his watch. 'Just about... now.'

The atmosphere of the sorting office changes at precisely ten o'clock. The CFC is switched off and the big machine clatters as it winds down. It hums and falls silent, but the noise is replaced by a new tension in the air.

Jenny flings an envelope into the South East box.

'That's it, kid. Grab your coat.'

She pitches another letter into the frame. 'I don't know, Roger. I can't really afford to lose the money right now.' She continues sorting at her usual pace as all around her men throw down their post and abandon their frames. She feels Roger watching her, but doesn't look up.

'None of these boys can,' he says. 'But you've

heard the union guys speak. We've got to stick together. Things will only get worse if we don't. Come on, take your things.' He grabs Jenny's coat from beneath the bench and holds it out to her. From all around the sorting office, men file past them on their way to the door.

She shakes her head. 'No. I think I'm going to stay on if it's all right with you.'

'You know, Jenny…' He keeps his voice low as he leans in close. 'Things could get ugly round here if you do.' He nods at a man leaving the floor. 'All right, Jim?' and waits until he's out of earshot before he speaks again. 'Things like this, they can get out of hand. Tempers flare. People feel betrayed. Some of these militant types can turn pretty nasty. I knew a bloke, years ago, who worked through a one-day strike over something like this. End of his shift, time to go home, he found the tyres on his car had been slashed. Men he'd worked with for twenty years turned against him. Just like that. Sent him to Coventry. Made his life miserable.'

Jenny pauses. 'What happened to him?'

'He's flying to Australia next month to see his grandkids.'

She reaches out and lightly touches Roger's arm. 'You?'

He shrugs his shoulders and laughs. 'I've been a diehard union man ever since. But there's still those round here who don't so much as give me the time of day. Some of these blokes have long memories. You need to be careful.'

She glances up at the security windows and wonders if there are people standing behind them, waiting to see what she'll do. She knows now that what she has to lose by walking out is greater than what she has to lose by staying. 'If you ask me, it sounds like there's thugs on both sides. Guess I'll just have to take my chances.'

Roger shakes his head. 'Kid, you're either brave or foolish. I don't know which.'

She nods and flings an envelope at her frame.

'Ah, bugger them.' Roger sighs and watches the last of the men leave the floor. 'Mickey's a bit of a crafty character, anyway.' He shoves Jenny's coat back under the bench and picks up a handful of letters. 'In another week, I'll be retired anyway. What do I care?'

*

The three of them are sitting at the kitchen table when she returns home from work in the afternoon. Charlotte and Ian are laughing as she walks in but fall silent when they see her and turn their attention to *The News* opened out on the table before them.

Jenny eases herself along the vinyl bench to sit next to Simon. Warily, she glances at her daughter.

'What are you all so happy about?' She cranes her neck to look at the paper. They've been going through the classifieds and have circled a number of ads.

'Nothing,' Charlotte says, folding the newspaper and pushing it to the far end of the table. Her smile looks as if it has been hammered into place.

Simon clears his throat. 'We've been talking, Jen.'

Already she does not like the sound of this. She studies Charlotte and Ian, pressed against each other on the opposite side of the table. Charlotte looks her in the eye, but Ian, Jenny can tell, is focusing to the left a little, at her ear maybe, or the picture on the wall behind her head. *Coward*, she thinks, then turns to Simon. 'Oh?'

'Thing is, the kids want a place of their own.'

Jenny feels the blood rising within her and wonders if the sound of her heartbeat pounds in their ears as it does in her own. She returns Charlotte's gaze but remains silent, certain that the child within the woman will show itself.

'I told you she'd be against it.' Charlotte folds her arms and shifts her eyes away from Jenny.

Simon lifts his hand. 'Just let me handle this, okay?' He turns to Jenny. 'Ian's already got a decent job, and if Charlotte increases her hours at Tesco they could easily afford to rent a little flat. Nothing fancy, but it would be a start.'

'Yeah,' Charlotte cuts in. 'My manager says I can go full-time whenever I want. There's plenty of work on the checkout.'

Jenny looks at Simon for support, then back at

her daughter. 'But what about university? If you lived at home and worked a year, you'd have a good nest egg saved up. If you rent a flat you'll have nothing to show for it.'

Charlotte sighs loudly and stares at her again. 'I've already told you, *Mother*. I'm not going.'

'Look, Jen.' Simon drums his fingers on the table top a couple of times, then presses his hand flat against the formica. 'I've been thinking. Maybe Charlotte's right. University isn't really for the likes of us. I mean, maybe she could go to the poly instead, maybe learn a trade, but why go filling her head with big ideas if it only leads to disappointment? We should be happy she wants to work.'

Jenny's mind is racing. Why is he saying this now? Doesn't he realise that if they don't stand together Charlotte will easily defeat them? She turns to him and lowers her voice. 'Shouldn't we talk about this in private?'

Across the table, Charlotte huffs. 'This is nothing to do with what *you* want, Mother. How many times do I have to tell you?'

Jenny's eyes dart from Simon to Charlotte and back again. 'But don't you see? Things would be so much better if she had a degree. It'll open doors for her. Isn't that what they say? She could have a proper career instead of just working to pay the bills like we've always had to do. It'll give her *choices* we could only dream about.'

Charlotte slams her fist on the table. 'Stop it,

Mother! Just stop it, would you. I don't know why you're making such a fuss over me now.'

Ian tries to interject. 'Maybe your mother's right, Char. Maybe we need to—'

'No,' Charlotte cuts him off. 'She's *not* right.'

She stares at Jenny. 'It was your perfect little Sophie who was going to achieve all your dreams. Not me. That was your plan, wasn't it? She was the smart one. Remember? I've just inherited your expectations by accident. Stop pretending you're doing any of this for my benefit.'

Jenny recoils at the venom in Charlotte's words and the cruelty with which she spits out her sister's name. She presses a hand to her throat. She can barely breathe.

Simon glares at Charlotte. 'Just let me handle this, all right?' He slides away from Jenny and looks her directly in the eyes for the first time since she sat down. 'I know how much this means to you, but a supermarket job is proper work. People always need to eat. If she doesn't want to go to university, we can't force her.'

'But I thought we were... I thought you said—'

Simon cuts in before she can finish her thought. 'People can change their minds, Jenny.'

She can see now that it's too late. Decisions have been made without her. There's nothing more she can do.

Across the table, Charlotte lifts her chin and glowers at her. The ring on her finger shines like a warning beacon. *Danger. Keep away.*

VI

It is Saturday morning, the start of the bank holiday weekend, and this time she is taking the car ferry to Fishbourne, a few miles to the west of Ryde. A veil of fog hangs over the water, and the seam between sea and sky, crafted anew each morning, is stitched so finely that from the bow of the ship Jenny cannot tell where one ends and the other begins. Everything is white and empty and thick with silence.

Lost in the mist somewhere off to the right of the ship, a foghorn cries out. A moment later, a muffled reply rises up on the left, and for a while they sing a mournful duet to the new day.

Jenny is nearly forty and she has never been abroad. Lately, she has begun to doubt that she will ever get another chance. Holidays with Simon and the girls were always taken within a day's coach ride of home, in Devon and Cornwall, or sometimes on the Isle of Wight. And once, when Charlotte and Sophie were still scrambling about on baby legs, they had gone to Blackpool for a week. She remembers the girls tottering along the beach at low tide and Simon pirouetting with them in turn, swinging them up to the sky and landing them safely on the wet sand.

Forty. If she's lucky, she still has half the lifetime that's been allotted to her – half or two-thirds or maybe three-quarters of which she will still be healthy and active and thankful to be alive; the rest – one-quarter or a third or maybe half, in decline, slowly at first, then more rapidly through illness or accident or wear and tear. Her eyes will become cloudy. Her hearing will fade. Her knuckles will swell and her knees and hips and back will ache. Whichever way she looks at it, the days in front of her are fewer than the days behind. In the past few years she has watched her mother grow thin and stooped, the bitterness condensing along with her body, and she has felt repulsed by what she too may one day become.

She has cycled round half of the island now. It has not been a thorough search, but she has done the best she could. Her best, though, has never quite been good enough. She could always have done better. Out there somewhere not far away, a girl pines for her lover, lost to her forever for all she knows, and now it's up to Jenny to show her the way to go forward. She needs to give her hope. She needs to give her purpose.

A clutch of scooters circles round her as the ferry glides into the dock at Fishbourne. When the ramp is lowered and they are released on to the island the scooters rev their motors and overtake her before her wheels have reached the tarmac. A thin stream of lorries and Ford Escorts follows along behind, speeding up and shifting and flowing past her as she grinds uphill through the long car park towards the road. When the vehicles slow into the junction she stands on the pedals and slots into position behind a transit van. Stuck to the van's rear doors are the flags of a dozen different countries, a bumper sticker from *The Best Little Campground in Teesside*, a lumbering moose, a Spanish bull, the Eiffel Tower, *Surf's up!* Inside, an Australian flag is draped across the back window like a curtain, and as the queue of vehicles joins the A3054 Jenny races after it.

Climbing up and into Wootton Bridge, she is comforted by how familiar this other world has become. And yet, its strangeness is exhilarating, too. Each day she spends here – each moment – is completely new, its conclusion as yet unknown. On the island, unlike at home, her future has not yet been written, and anything at all is possible. Right now, there is nowhere else she would rather be. Turning left, away from the village, she climbs through the back lanes to Staplers Hill and feels the blood racing through her veins again.

When she reaches the top, she stops at the side of the road and watches this new world emerge from the mist. If she could, she would bottle this moment and share it with Simon and Charlotte. *How she would love to give them a sip of this freedom!* – the feeling that the world outside this precise moment and this exact spot does not exist. Not Taylor or Mickey Jones or Ian or Mrs Thatcher. Not yesterday or tomorrow. Only now. Only this place. Only her and this road and her bicycle.

She has passed through Newport once before, checking the phone directory and making a cursory search for Edward Cottages on her way into and out of town. The hunt had only just begun then, and August had stretched out in front of her abundant with time. She'd been certain of the success of her mission. Now, though, after the weeks have slipped by without the merest reward for her efforts she feels a sense of urgency. Time is running out. Then, as she turns into the high street she sees it – the café on the corner with the red gingham curtains. She has an ally here, the romantic young girl, so eager to help with her search.

'Jenny!' The girl greets her like an old friend as she steps through the door. It is early still, and the café is quiet. Just one man in the corner, reading the *Daily Express* over a cup of coffee and the remnants of his breakfast. 'I knew you'd come back!' Lily waves through the hatch into the kitchen. 'Nan! It's Jenny. She's come back.' And soon they are sitting in the corner with a pot of tea and three cups on the table.

Nan pours the tea and passes the jug of milk to Jenny. 'Lily here has been hoping you'd come by this way again. She's got everyone in town on the hunt for your Miss Cunningham.'

The girl pulls a small notebook from the pocket of her apron and slides it across the table. 'I've been keeping a record of everyone I ask.'

Jenny touches the front of the notebook and opens it to the first page. 'These are the people who came into the café the day you were here. See, there's Mrs Bamber and Mrs Morris. Remember them? They come after church every Sunday and sit over there.' She points to the table in the window, where Jenny had sat that day and where the old man now reads his paper. 'Except they sat over there the day you came in.' She points again to the next table over.

Nan shakes her head and laughs. 'I swear. The girl has a photographic memory. I don't know how she does it.'

Barely two weeks have passed since Jenny was here – *How many people have sat at that table since?* – but the notebook is nearly full. 'I... I don't know what to say.'

Lily's handwriting has the precision of a schoolgirl, with its looping Ls and Gs, and each letter is perfectly formed. The only deviation from one day to the next is the colour of ink. 'I use a different pen every day so it's easy to tell them apart.' There are three pages of blue at the beginning of the book on the Sunday when Jenny began her search, and four pages of red on Monday, changing to purple on Tuesday, and pink on Wednesday. On Thursdays and Fridays the writing changes to thin, bird-like scratchings written in black, the letters falling haphazardly above and below the lines.

'Ah, now that's me,' Nan says, looking over Jenny's shoulder. 'I take over on the days when Lily isn't working. But she's given me very clear instructions.' Nan pats Lily's hand. 'Haven't you, love?'

Jenny reads a page of red out loud:

'Two ladies visiting aunt: no

'Mr Piper: no

'Old man with hat: no

'Family from mainland: no

'Mr and Mrs Johnson: will ask their daughter

'Tommy F and Mum: no

'Table of tourists: no

'Mrs Anderson: will ask neighbours

'Mr and Mrs Singh: will ask children'

'Do you see how it works?' Lily flicks a few pages ahead to a pink day. 'Mr and Mrs Johnson popped in for tea and scones a couple of days later.' She draws her finger down the page and finds their names. 'There they are. "Mr and Mrs Johnson: daughter doesn't know the name but will ask around." And a few days later they returned again.' She looks up at Jenny. 'They're regulars, here: "still looking". There must be thirty or forty people now who are helping with the search.'

'Pretty impressive, isn't she, our little Lily, here?'

Just then, the bell above the door jangles and a young couple step inside. They hesitate a moment before choosing a table with a view looking out at the side street.

'And what about you, love? I guess you're still looking for Deborah, too.'

Jenny nods. 'Yes, I'm still looking, though I'm afraid my method can't compete with Lily's.' She smiles at the young girl. 'If I could clone you and set you to work around the island I think we would find her in no time.'

Lily keeps an eye on the young couple at the side table, and when they have had time to look at the menu she stands and smooths her apron. 'I don't recognise them,' she whispers. 'You never know, they could be Deborah's next-door neighbours. I'll go and ask.'

Nan chuckles softly as she and Jenny watch Lily cross the room to take the couple's order. 'She's a little star, that one. I don't know what I'll do without her. She's back to school next week and my regular girl is back from her hols.'

The bell rings again and a family enters. A couple with two teenaged children and their gran.

Nan pushes her chair away from the table. 'Looks like I better get back to the kitchen.' She places a hand on Jenny's shoulder and gives it a gentle squeeze. 'Good luck with your search, love.'

Jenny watches Lily as she writes the young couple's order on her notepad, then stops to exchange a few more words before moving on. She imagines Lily is quizzing them about Deborah, urging them to search their memories for the name. She might be someone from their schooldays, or a friend of a friend they once met. Someone has got to know her. The couple talk between themselves a moment, then finally the woman shakes her head.

Lily glances at Jenny as she passes to the back of the room. 'Two full English,' she calls through the hatch to Nan.

As Lily moves on to the table of five, Jenny turns to the last page in the notebook. *Saturday 25 August.* Today. There are just a handful of entries so far, including *Old man with walking stick: no,* and *Mr Thompson: no.* She glances towards the man sitting at the window table on his own. Mr Thompson, she decides. Beneath his entry, Jenny writes her own. *Young couple, Full English: no.*

It is mid-morning now, and the café is getting busy. Jenny scribbles a note on a piece of paper with her telephone number and presses it into Lily's hand on her way to the door. 'Thank you.'

Out on the street again, she sees the police station on the next corner. In some respects, Deborah Cunningham is indeed a missing person. No one has seen her. No one knows where she is. Surely the police could help in the search. But then she remembers – she has not committed a simple misdemeanour but an actual crime. *Mail theft.* There's more at stake than just her job.

Deborah is so close now that Jenny is certain she can feel her presence. On her way out of town she stops at a zebra crossing and watches a young woman cross the road. Briefly, she catches her eye. Was that her? Or is she the woman in the blue mini pulling out of the side road up ahead? Or the girl who gazes back at her from the window of a bus as it passes?

The streets and side streets are empty as she rolls through Calbourne. There are no dog walkers, no neighbours chatting over garden hedges, no farm tractors idling on the side of the road at the edge of the village. No one to speak to and ask for advice. Jenny hesitates at a fork in the road and examines her map again. Maybe she should have turned earlier, up one of the narrow tracks west of Parkhurst. Her heart thumps in her chest. There are so many little lanes on her map. Which is the right one to choose? She takes a deep breath to steady her nerves and think again. She cannot possibly ride them all. But that was never the plan. So, here she is. Shalfeet or Newbridge? Neither is very big, but who's to say where Deborah waits? Weaving her way through both, Jenny loops back on herself to pick up Ningwood and Wellow, then Thorley Street and Thorley before dropping down to the sea again at Bouldnor.

She had been surprised by just how easy it was to fall in love with Simon, and the speed at which love struck had made her doubt the feelings she'd had for Paolo. After all, the two men couldn't have been more different. Paulo was dark and moody and mysterious and complex, while Simon was down to earth and straightforward. Paolo was confident, and always had something interesting to say. Simon often appeared awkward and struggled to find his words. Paolo had educated himself and he wanted to educate her, but Simon had no grand plan for his life or any desire to mould her into something other than what she already was. Paolo had wanted the world and he went off to find it, while Simon had simpler wants and simpler expectations. A job. A home. A family. *Her*. It was a different kind of love, of course, for Simon lacked Paolo's unpredictability. But surprises were no longer an appeal. What she wanted, then, was what she'd never had: a feeling of rootedness; of security; of really and truly belonging to someone; of knowing what the future held before it happened.

It is mid-afternoon by the time she reaches Yarmouth, and the town centre is busy with day-trippers and clusters of the shiny scooters that had rolled off the ferry with her that morning. The air is clear now, and from the common she can see across the Solent to the mainland. If she turned around now, she could circle back to Fishbourne and be home in time for tea. But the sun is still high overhead. She checks her watch. There's time to go a bit further.

*

Evening catches her on the western edge of the island, where the cliffs break apart and tumble into the sea. With the rhythmic turning of the wheels, she had lost track of the passage of time and of the movement of the sun in the sky. Each bend in the road and each new lane up ahead held the possibility of finding Deborah. She'd begun to think that as long as she continued to pedal, the sun would continue to shine. And all the while it did, she kept going, pedalling further and further, ignoring the lengthening shadows, putting off the moment she would have to turn back. At last, on the cliffs above Alum Bay she comes to a stop. There, she watches the sun kiss the horizon and begin to melt into the sea.

As daylight fades into dusk a neon bulb flickers into life not far from where she stands, illuminating a guest house sign: Sunnybank Lodge. In the west, clouds burst into flame with the setting sun and reflect in the windows of the lodge. Fifty yards up the road, a telephone box glows in the dusk. She goes to it, leans her bicycle against it, and pulls from her pocket the list of phone numbers she has collected along the way. She dials the numbers, one by one, then finally dials her own.

'So you've left, then? Just like that?' His voice is soft but the words feel sharp when they touch her ear.

'No, of course not,' she says quickly. 'That wasn't my intention. I just came to the island to clear my head. I don't even have a change of clothes. But there's something I need to do, here. I can't explain. I don't understand it myself.'

'Right,' he says. 'And when exactly do you think you will?'

Silence is so much easier than this.

'I just need some time to think,' she says, then before she can stop herself the words tumble from her lips. 'I don't want us to go on as we have been, Si. I really can't do it any more. Things need to change. You know it, too.'

He laughs. 'And this is your way of making things better? Running off without a word to anyone?'

She presses her forehead against a pane of glass. It feels cool against her skin. 'I haven't run off. I promise. I wouldn't leave Charlotte like that.'

She hears the sharp intake of breath and imagines his face, jaw set firm, eyes closed.

'And what about me?' he says, softly. 'Are you leaving me?'

In her pocket, her fingers wrap round another ten-pence piece but she leaves the coin where it is. 'I love you, Si. You have to believe that.' The words sound hollow, but she wants to believe them, too.

'You've got a funny way of showing it,' he whispers before the telephone beeps and the line falls silent.

'So have you.'

*

Morning filters through the bay window and fills the dining room with a pale light. All but one of the tables is occupied and as she steps through the door she casts her eyes around for somewhere to sit. For the first time in years she has slept past sunrise, and a new day has started without her. She sits alone at a table with four chairs, surrounded by couples and tables of friends who casually pass comments about *throttle linkage connections* and *reed valve tuning* around the room. In the corner a middle-aged man wearing drainpipe trousers and winklepicker shoes sits opposite a woman with a blonde Chelsea cut. Bowed over their breakfast, they talk softly in indecipherable tones, looking up now and then to join a conversation about carburettors or chrome restoration.

Jenny helps herself to coffee and cereal from the counter that runs along the wall, and before she has finished her cornflakes the room begins to clear. The stairs creak as people return to their rooms to collect their coats, and a few minutes later the stairs creak again as they prepare to leave.

A man in a fishtail parka stops at the dining-room door and calls through the room to the adjoining kitchen. 'Thanks, Mrs N. See you tonight.'

The landlady emerges from the kitchen carrying Jenny's breakfast. 'See you tonight, you lot. Have fun.'

The woman sets the plate in front of Jenny: a sausage and a strip of bacon lay side by side; two eggs, their yellow discs closed over by milky cataracts; triangles of golden fried bread; half a tomato, its skin puckered from the frying pan. A generous mound of baked beans spreads slowly across the plate, binding the rest together.

Outside in the driveway, the scooters rev to life one by one. Horns beep farewell as tyres crunch through the gravel to the road. Mrs Newman crosses the room and stands at the bay window watching them leave as a younger woman clears plates from the empty tables and disappears back into the kitchen.

'There's toast as well,' the landlady says when she turns back to the room. She points to a loaf of sliced bread and a toaster on the counter. 'As much as you like.'

Jenny nods. 'Thanks,' she says. 'I guess I'll need it. It's a long way home.' She ends the sentence with a smile, though the shape of it feels tight and awkward on her mouth.

Mrs Newman laughs. 'When you showed up last night and said you were on a bike, I assumed you meant a scooter. I thought you'd got yourself separated from the others. I couldn't believe it when I saw your pushbike.' She continues to hover by Jenny's table, attentive and maternal, then asks, 'Mind if I join you?' She slides her bulky frame into the opposite chair before Jenny has time to respond. 'I hope you don't mind me saying, but it seems like you could do with the company.'

Jenny offers another feeble smile.

'Go ahead, love. Eat your breakfast.'

Jenny cuts a corner off a piece of the fried bread, runs it through the tomato sauce, and knifes a few beans on to the back of her fork. She chews, self-consciously, eyes focused on the plate rather than her companion.

'The August bank holiday weekend is my favourite part of the summer. All the young ones – and the not-so-young ones – out there on their motor scooters. They're certainly a colourful lot. I look forward to it all year long.' She sighs, heavily. 'But I dread it as well. The scooter rally marks the end of the season hereabouts. Come next week, and things will start to get quiet.' She glances around the room. The plates have all been cleared away now, and fresh cutlery laid in readiness for the next morning.

'The kiddies will be back at school in a week or so, and things will slow right down. I used to enjoy having a rest after all the commotion of the summer, but the winter season gets awfully lonely now that Mr Newman's gone.'

She brushes a wrinkle from the table linen and nods to the girl tidying up the coffee counter at the side. 'You can go once the dishes are done. I'll take care of the rest.'

She turns back to Jenny. 'I miss the summer guests when they're gone. People come alive when they're on holiday, don't you think? They forget their worries and relax, and they're not afraid to let you see them smile from time to time. And I miss Mr Newman, too, of course.' She gazes out the window. 'We made quite a team, the two of us.'

'It's hard on your own, isn't it?' Jenny looks into Mrs Newman's eyes. They are blue and friendly, but they glisten with recent sadness.

'You've lost your husband, too?'

Jenny shakes her head and prods a piece of fried bread with her fork. 'No. Not yet, anyway.' She sighs, then adds, 'I don't know, maybe I already have and just don't know it.' She is not used to confessing her problems to strangers, but she continues. 'Things at home haven't been so good, lately.'

Mrs Newman reaches across the table and touches Jenny's hand. 'Sometimes life gets hard. I know.' The woman's hand is warm and soft, and the gesture brings tears to Jenny's eyes.

'Mr Newman and me, we weren't without our troubles, either. I refused to talk to him for six whole months when the children were small. He had a lady friend, you see.'

Jenny is quick to defend her husband. 'Simon hasn't done anything like that. I couldn't forgive him if he had.' There have been times, though, when she has almost wished he'd been unfaithful, wished for a legitimate reason to hate him, a reason to leave and start again. 'But you stayed?'

'Divorce wasn't the done thing in those days, you have to remember. Some women had to put up with a whole lot worse than I did. Besides, I had three little ones to think about. Didn't have much choice but to stay and work things out. So that's what I did.'

Mrs Newman chuckles softly. 'You'd be surprised at the things a person can forgive when they want to. It's a choice, you know – forgiveness. I hated what he did, and it's true, I hated him for a time. But we had a history together. We had children.

And despite what he'd done, I did still love him. Human beings are fallible creatures, love. We're all struggling in one way or another, and trying to do the best we can.'

Jenny lifts her head and looks at Mrs Newman.

'After six months, I said to myself, "Dorothy, you can either go on floundering about in this cesspool of silence or you can swim to the edge and pull yourself out. The choice is yours." I sat down to supper that evening and I said, "Would you pass the salt, please, Harry?" Honest to God, those were the first words I'd spoken to him in all that time.'

'What did he say?'

'He asked if I wanted the pepper pot, too.' She chuckles to herself and gazes out the bay window at the sea.

Jenny thinks of Simon at home now, in that empty house on his own. What would become of him if she left? What would become of her? They, too, had a history together. Would all the pain they shared finally be healed if they parted? Or would another injury just be added to the rest?

'Harry's been gone just over two years now. He went real sudden. Heart attack. If you've got to go, I guess that's the way to do it. Fast. Without any lingering about. But it was a terrible shock. And now, after forty years, I'm on my own. The children all moved away. And the grandchildren are nearly grown now, and getting ready to move even further afield. They all come back to the island for a week at

Christmas, but they've got their own lives now. And I can't blame them for that, can I? Isn't that why we spend so much time raising them? So they don't need us in the end?'

Mrs Newman turns her face back to the window and gazes into the distance. 'The New World is out there, if you travel far enough. That's what they tell me, anyway.'

*

The two women stand in the doorway, watching the wind blow through the tops of the trees in the garden. There's a chill in the air, but the sky overhead is clear now and sunlight glistens off the dew-headed lawn. If Jenny ignores the dark band of cloud that hangs on the western horizon it looks to be a perfect morning for a bicycle ride.

'Are you sure you want to go, love? The weather report says we're in for heavy rain, this afternoon. I could put your bicycle in the boot of the car and have you back to Fishbourne within the hour.'

Jenny squeezes Mrs Newman's hand. 'I need to get on,' she says. 'Besides, the wind is going my way. I'll be home in no time.' She wheels her bicycle on to the driveway, waves to Mrs Newman and pushes off.

'Wait! Just a minute!' Mrs Newman disappears back inside the guest house for a moment, then hurries down the steps with an orange mac in her hands.

'Take this.' She holds the jacket up and gives it a shake. 'It was Harry's. It's a bit big, but you might need it before the day's over. You can bring it back another time and tell me how things turn out.'

The woman folds the jacket and places it in the handlebar basket, beneath the sandwiches and the fruit cake she has packed for Jenny's lunch. 'There,' she says. 'You'll be okay now.' She puts a heavy arm around Jenny's shoulders and hugs her briefly. 'You better get going.'

At the end of the drive, Jenny glances back at the house and waves one last time before turning into the lane and feeling the wind push up behind her.

The old road from the Needles to Freshwater Bay rolls along in waves as if the land were a solid sea, cresting and falling with a frozen tide. The sea itself has turned a steely grey, white horses punctuating its surface as it churns in the wind. As she joins the A3055 again, following along the southern coast, she catches glimpses of the chalk cliffs crumbling into the waves. The whole island, it seems, is being consumed by the sea.

She keeps to the edge of the road, squeezed between the grassy verge and the last of the summer holiday traffic. Now and then, as she climbs the long hill to the top of Military Road, moving slowly in her lowest gear, cars grow impatient and push past too close. She keeps her eyes focused on the tarmac and presses on, holding a straight line and holding her nerve. A string of scooters follows her uphill, overtaking her, one by one, and tooting their horns in encouragement as they slowly pull past. Jenny has learned to ride the hills now, learned when to shift down and when to shift up, and how to use the momentum of the downhills to carry her up the next incline. And with the wind behind her, she no longer needs to stop and push.

As she reaches the top and picks up speed, she shifts into a higher gear and soon she is racing along the top of the cliffs. Nothing and no one passes her now. Over her shoulder, the Channel spreads wide. Out there is France, and beyond France is Spain, and beyond Spain is the whole continent of Africa. She tries to imagine these other worlds, tries to imagine herself in them, on her own and with Simon. If she asked him, would he go?

At Brookgreen, above Brook Bay, she turns inland to follow a seam of villages: Brightstone, Shorwell and Chale Green. She makes cursory stops along the way, out of habit and obligation. Then, it is back to the coast to Chale and Blackgang Chine.

*

On the cliffs above Blackgang Chine, she finds a bench facing out to sea and unwraps the lunch Mrs Newman packed for her that morning: cheese and pickle sandwiches made with thick slices of soft white bread, a slice of fruit cake, a Cox's orange pippin. If she thinks back far enough, she can almost remember a time when her mother sent her off to school with lunches such as this, layered with love and affection – food that provided far more than sustenance. And when was the last time she provided Simon and Charlotte with that kind of care?

The cliff where she sits looking out to sea is familiar. They have been here once before, she remembers, she and Simon and the girls, back when Charlotte and Sophie were still sparrow-boned and so buoyant she thought they might actually be able to fly. Together, the girls had held hands and danced about the grassy plateau, their giddy laughter filling the air as they spun round and round so long and so fast that Jenny had feared they would break free of the earth and soar away without her. She lets the memory rest upon her for a moment. She and Simon had been happy back then, with everything in the world they had wanted right there in front of them.

On the horizon, out at sea, diagonal streaks of grey slice through the sky. Jenny doesn't linger over her food as she would have liked, but balls up the waxed paper from the sandwich and returns the fruit cake and the apple to her basket. The clouds are pulling in now, gathering together, and the air is thick with the earthy scent of the approaching rain. If she is to have a chance of missing the storm she must move quickly.

But memories of this place and that other life and Mrs Newman's kindness are too much. Before she can turn away from them, she is crying. And the dampness of the tears makes her think not of the rain that is coming but of blood. She sees Sophie and Charlotte dancing away from her, out of reach. She hears their laughter recede. Simon, too, is withdrawing from her, pulling further and further away until he is gone. Then earth and sky and sea spin together like the petals of a pinwheel and the edge of the cliff races to her feet. There, she hovers between sea and sky as her lungs spasm and strain to draw breath. Without air, she is dizzy and weightless. One step forward and she, too, could fly.

As the sea and sky reach out to her she clutches her chest. She gasps for air but it does not come. Seagulls swoop and scream overhead, and still she cannot breathe. Then all of the hurt and shame and regret and fury she has guarded so carefully since Sophie's death rise to the surface. She falls to her knees, panting, as the gulls dive closer, their shrill cries piercing the air. Folding her arms over her head, she awaits the crash.

It was no one's fault. How many times has she heard those words? *No one is to blame.* That's what they told her: the police, the doctors, Simon. Even her mother had said it was an accident, that she mustn't blame herself.

The evening had been dark and the road was wet. Rain; a dog or a fox darting across the street; a distracted girl who didn't look up in time: it was *an accident* they said. It was no one's fault. The driver wasn't speeding. He wasn't drunk. He wasn't having an affair or an argument with the woman in the passenger seat. He simply did not see the girl step off the pavement on her way to the corner shop to buy eggs for her mother. It was no one's fault. That's what they said. But Jenny knew the truth.

'Can't you just do this one thing for me?' She seldom raised her voice to her daughters but she had shouted at Sophie that night in the kitchen. The next day was Charlotte's seventeenth birthday and Jenny was making a cake. But she had forgotten to buy eggs and 'dammit all, Sophie! You can't make a cake without eggs!'

In the kitchen, the windows were fogged with the steam of boiling carrots and new potatoes, and she had wedged them open to let in the fresh air. Simon would be home soon and dinner was nearly ready.

'Don't argue with me. Hurry up! Just do it! Go!' Then the front door slammed shut and Sophie was gone.

Minutes later, the screech of car tyres and a soft, almost silent thud had travelled on the breeze through the window, to her ear. Tyres often squealed round corners, she told herself as she turned off the tap and went to set the water jug on the table. Cars skidded at junctions and roundabouts all the time.

It wasn't until the siren had screamed its way down the street, its blue light stopping at the corner to pulse like a heartbeat through her net curtains that she looked at the clock above the stove. Sophie should have been home by now. Why was she taking so long? Didn't she know she needed those eggs?

*

The rain arrives as she reaches the edge of Niton. It is a misty, drizzly sort of rain that hangs in the air and over time is no less damp than a downpour. It drips off her chin and runs down her neck, and seeps through the seams of Mr Newman's rain coat. Soon she will be soaked through.

The road forks, then forks again. Signs point to Godshill and Newport and home in one direction, and St Lawrence and Ventnor in the other. She has been to Ventnor already, but turning inland now would leave a gap large enough for Deborah to slip through. More than anything, she wants to go home. But St Lawrence is only three miles away and she has come so far already. She cannot quit now.

The sea is the same colour as the wet tarmac beneath her wheels, but while the road is smooth and glides gently through the hills, the sea rises in angry waves that fall and spring up again in an urgent churning of the waters of the world. Jenny thinks again about the lilo floating to Australia. In weather like this it would be lost out there, capsized, washed up in Sydney Harbour, months from now, its cargo plundered by the storm.

She rolls into St Lawrence, down past the houses and down past the shops, watching the sea grow nearer again. It is Sunday afternoon and the rain has emptied the streets. Everyone is home now, tucked up in the dry and the warm. She pictures them within the soft glow of their living rooms, assembled round dining tables and fires and loved ones.

A single splash of red in an otherwise grey and gloomy street catches her eye. A phone box. Inside, Jenny shelters from the rain, gazing through the spotted windowpanes. She watches the droplets run down the glass, streaking and twisting the world outside before splitting again into a million prisms of light. Her father once gave her a cardboard kaleidoscope and when she had held it to her eye and rotated the end, it shattered the world into a galaxy of stars. Now and then, in the lifetime since he left, Jenny has taken the kaleidoscope from her dressing table drawer, held it to her eye and tried to coax the disassembled pieces to come together once more.

She pulls the *Woman's Own* from a plastic bag in her basket. The rain has found its way through the folds and the smiling woman on the cover is wet to the touch. The postcard was tucked safely between the centre pages of the magazine but damp has reached there, too, softening the corners so they bend in her hands. The picture, though, is not damaged and she turns the card over to look at it again. There it is. The beach hut. The endless miles of golden sand. The solitude is as familiar to her as the silent rooms of her own home. That was what had first drawn her to it and what makes her shiver now. Closely, she examines the shack at the far end of the beach. If someone is there, they sit alone, not in restful isolation but in exile. She wants to shout at them now to come out, to leave the hut and walk down the beach and return to civilisation. She wonders if it is Michael who is there and in her mind she urges him to break free.

Rain drips from the hood of Harry Newman's jacket, spotting the page of Cs in the telephone directory. There is a Cullwick, two Cummings and a Cundall in the area around St Lawrence, but not a single Cunningham. Jenny closes her eyes. She wishes she could go to sleep, but knows that her job here is not quite finished. She finds the last of her coins and dials her own number in Portsmouth.

On the other end of the line, the phone rings. Once, twice, three times. She looks at her watch. It is half past three on a rainy Sunday afternoon. She pictures the telephone in the corner of the sitting room, ringing into an empty space, and fears there is no one there to answer her call. But she continues to hang on, listening to this little strand of sound that is the only thing that seems to connect her with home, and knows she doesn't want to break this fragile tie. She will hang on for as long as it takes for someone to answer.

She holds the receiver in place with her shoulder and unfolds the map. She knows every road on the island except for this one, the one which will carry her home. Measuring the distance from St Lawrence to Fishbourne, her fingers march across the page in hurried strides: two and a half; five; seven and a half; ten; twelve miles back to the ferry. She could be there by five o'clock, and home by six.

She loses track of the number of times the telephone rings. Then, suddenly, it stops.

'Jenny, is that you?' Simon's voice is breathless. Even... desperate.

'Yes,' she whispers, wary of saying more – afraid he will put the phone down and break the delicate thread that holds them together.

He is silent, too, but she is comforted by the sound of his breathing and feels his breath spread out and fill the phone box.

At last, Simon breaks the silence. 'I've been thinking, Jen.' His voice shakes with emotion. 'You're right. We can't go on this way.'

She closes her eyes and braces herself against the panes of glass. 'We can't change what's happened. But we don't have to let it destroy us. Come back to me, Jenny. Please.'

She presses her hand against her mouth. She wants to tell him how sorry she is. For Sophie, for Charlotte, for the way she has shut him out these past two years. There is so much she needs to say. But the words pile up behind her tongue and block her voice.

She takes a breath. And then another. And slowly the words begin to settle into place. 'How can I?' she whispers. 'With everything I've done. How can you ever forgive me?'

She imagines him there, alone in their house, cradling the phone to his ear. 'I love you, Jenny. I always have and I always will. There's nothing to forgive.'

She brushes her fingers across a pane of breath-clouded glass. Rivulets of water wash away the misty curtain and the street outside the phone box comes into focus again.

She climbs the hill away from St Lawrence, putting all of her weight and all of her strength into making the pedals turn and turn again, just one more time before she is forced to stop and finish the climb on foot. It is a short, steep hill and she is winded when she reaches the top, but she is not defeated.

She doesn't stop in Whitwell, but rides past the post office and the pub and out the other end of the village. She rides fast and strong now, speeding along the rolling hills, dropping down to Godshill and on to Downend. With every mile she rides, the pull towards home becomes stronger.

Finally, at Wootton Bridge, she stops and plants both feet firmly on the ground. The wind has brought the clouds and scattered them again, clearing the early evening air. Light gleams off the still damp surfaces of the road and the grass and the houses and the trees, intensifying their colours and making the town pulse with life.

On a bench looking across the village pond, she sits and pours the lukewarm remnants of the morning from her flask and unfolds her map one last time. She traces a finger in loops and zigzags across the island. She has covered it all now, cycled through every town and nearly every village. And still she has not found Deborah.

She takes the magazine from the plastic carrier bag and pulls the postcard from its pages. Holding the card before her, she looks again at the colourful stamps in the corner and the shape of Deborah's name. It is nearly the end of the month now, just a few days from Michael's deadline, and she imagines him waiting by a phone that is never going to ring. She pictures Deborah, somewhere on the island, shattered by Michael's silence. *If I don't hear from you by then, I'll know it's really over.*

She shakes her head. 'No,' she says aloud, to herself as much as to Michael. 'It doesn't work like that. You don't just give up and say it's over unless you want it to be. There's always a way to make things right again.'

She knows at last that Paolo didn't leave her. She'd chosen to stay behind just as she'd chosen to marry Simon. Paolo had the choice of coming back, but didn't. Simon had the choice of leaving. And Charlotte, the result of all those choices, will be the creator of her own future, too. She and Ian will be whatever they decide to become.

Turning the card over once more, Jenny studies the picture. There's no one in the beach hut. She is certain of that now. In the sand above the tidemark, dimples of activity dot the beach. The footprints have been there all along, but only now does she see them, their edges smoothed by the breeze, striding away from the lonely little shack.

From the high street at the edge of the green, a red pillar box beckons. She shifts her position on the bench and tilts her head away, but still the postbox is there in the corner of her eye as she reads Michael's words again. The regret, the love – the message is heartfelt and full of passion. But if he really loves her – and if she still loves him – he won't read into her silence what isn't there. He will try and keep on trying to win her back.

And what about her and Simon? Mile after mile, she has tried to imagine her life without him. And she has failed. He is as much a part of who she is as her own heartbeat. He is her past, and she wants him to be her future.

The time has come.

She refolds the map and shakes a few drops of cold tea from her cup, then screws it back on to the flask and places the flask and the map and the magazine into the basket. Clasping the postcard between thumb and index finger she wheels the bicycle towards the waiting pillar box. For weeks, she has dreaded this moment; has imagined it as another failure. But now that it has arrived she is surprised by how easy it is. She is ready to go home.

Tomorrow is Charlotte's birthday and Roger's last day at work. If she goes home now, she can bake them each a cake and try to find all of the words she has saved to tell them how much they mean to her. Simon, too. Especially him. She knows she can't go back and begin again, but she can try – and keep on trying – to go forward, and to do things better in the future.

She holds the postcard to the lip of the letter box, then opens her fingers and lets it fall from her hand.

Acknowledgements

I would like to thank the wonderful team at Fairlight Books, especially Urška Vidoni who was my first reader there, and who having read a portion asked to read the whole. Thank you for your kind words of encouragement, your expert eye, and the gentle nudges that helped the story develop beyond what I thought it could. I'm very grateful, too, for the expertise of Charlotte Norman in dotting the 'i's and crossing the 't's, and for the advice and assistance of Bradley Thomas.

I would also like to thank my talented and inspirational friends, mentors and former colleagues at the University of Chichester. In particular, I am grateful to Karen Stevens, who was there at the beginning and encouraged me to continue, and to Alison MacLeod whose boundless enthusiasm urged me forward.

Drafts of this story have been in and out of my desk drawer numerous times over the past few years, and writer friends have generously volunteered their time to read and offer encouragement along the way. Laura Pearson was an early reader who astutely weeded out errant Americanisms, and more recently, Ellie Piddington's advice and suggestions helped me to see new possibilities. I am especially grateful to my dear friends Kate Leader and Barbara Grunwell whose belief and encouragement over the years has never wavered. It's my turn to buy lunch. Gaby Prichard, too, has been a marvellous source of encouragement. All of you have helped to keep the story alive in my imagination.

I am also thankful for my friendship with former posties Jane and Shaun Townsend, who never tired of my questions about the inner workings of the sorting office. Finally, I will forever be grateful to my mother, Karen Murray, whose early sacrifices make all things possible, and to my husband, Chris, who keeps my wheels turning and makes life an adventure.

Book club and writers' circle notes for the
Fairlight Moderns can be found at
www.fairlightmoderns.com

Share your thoughts about the book
with #MissingWordsNovella

Also in the Fairlight Moderns series

DOUGLAS BRUTON

Blue Postcards

Once there was a street in Paris and it was called the Street of Tailors. This was years back, in the blue mists of memory.

Now it's the 1950s and Henri is the last tailor on the street. With meticulous precision he takes the measurements of men and notes them down in his leather-bound ledger. He draws on the cloth with a blue chalk, cuts the pieces and sews them together. When the suit is done, Henri adds a finishing touch: a blue Tekhelet thread hidden in the trousers somewhere, for luck. One day, the renowned French artist Yves Klein walks into the shop, and orders a suit.

'*Seductively original, linguistically daring, almost dangerously immersive.*'
—Stephen May, author of the Costa shortlisted *Life! Death! Prizes!*

'Blue Postcards *is an expertly written, evocative tale of love and loss.*'
—Julie Corbin, author of
A Lie For A Lie

JT TORRES

Taking Flight

When Tito is a child, his grandmother teaches
him how to weave magic around the ones
you love in order to keep them close.

She is the master and he is the pupil, exasperating
Tito's put-upon mother who is usually the focus of
their mischief.

As Tito grows older and his grandmother's mind
becomes less sound, their games take a dangerous
turn. They both struggle with a particular spell, one
that creates an illusion of illness to draw in love.
But as the lines between magic and childish tales
blur, so too do those between fantasy and reality.

'Taking Flight *is a finely crafted,
lyrical song of a book.*'
—Amy Kurzweil, author of *Flying
Couch: a graphic memoir*

'*The exquisite writing of JT Torres is on full
display in this deftly told and spellbinding tale.*'
—Don Rearden, author of
The Raven's Gift